PUFFIN B

TOM TI

It's the summer holidays and Vic and his best friend, Brian,
are looking for something to do. That's when they spot the
plastic rowing-boat in the workshop where Vic's dad works
and manage to persuade him to let them borrow it. It's only
the size of a bathtub but it's big enough to go exploring on
the canal. The only problem is that Sam and her little sister,
Mary-Lou, have to go with them – and then Darryl follows
them too, which is not what Vic and Brian had in mind for
their adventure at all! Together they discover the perfect
place for a den – an abandoned canal boat moored off
wasteland known locally as Tom Tiddler's Ground. But ap-
parently they're not the only ones interested in the old
wreck. It seems they've stumbled on to a fifty-year-old mys-
tery of murder and lost treasure which they've got to solve
before it's too late.

John Rowe Townsend took an Honours degree at Cam-
bridge, then worked for several years as a journalist, mainly
on the *Guardian*. He has written more than twenty books
for children and young people, and a definitive history of
children's books, *Written for Children*. The awards he has re-
ceived include the Boston Globe Hornbook Prize. He has
lectured on books for children in this country, the USA,
Canada, Australia and Japan.

John Rowe Townsend

TOM TIDDLER'S GROUND

Illustrated by Mark Peppé

Puffin Books

PUFFIN BOOKS

Published by the Penguin Group
Penguin Books Ltd, 27 Wrights Lane, w8 5TZ, England
Viking Penguin, a division of Penguin Books USA Inc.
375 Hudson Street, New York, New York 10014, USA
Penguin Books Australia Ltd, Ringwood, Victoria, Australia
Penguin Books Canada Ltd, 2801 John Street, Markham, Ontario, Canada L3R 1B4
Penguin Books (NZ) Ltd, 182–190 Wairau Road, Auckland 10, New Zealand

Penguin Books Ltd, Registered Offices: Harmondsworth, Middlesex, England

First published by Viking Kestrel 1985
Published in Puffin Books 1987
10 9 8 7 6 5 4 3 2

Copyright © John Rowe Townsend, 1985
Illustrations copyright © Mark Peppé, 1985
All rights reserved

Printed in England by Clays Ltd, St Ives plc
Typeset in Baskerville

Here we come on Tom Tiddler's Ground,
Picking up gold and silver.

LINES CHANTED BY CHILDREN
IN AN OLD GAME

1

It was last summer it all happened. It started when me and Brain first saw the plastic rowing-boat, about the size of a bathtub, that my dad had taken in part exchange for a motor-bike. And that was three or four days after school broke up for the long holiday.

You know how it is. We'd been looking forward to the end of term, and saying, 'Only another two weeks,' then, 'Only another week,' then, 'Only four days more,' and so on. And then the day came, and it was all over, and we'd left Claypits Primary for good, because we were moving on to the Comprehensive next term. And a few days after that we were fed up and looking for something to do.

Brain is my best friend. His real name is Brian, but when he was little he always got the letters the wrong way round and spelled it Brain. So we called him that. The funny thing is, he *is* brainy. Maybe a name does something for you. I wish mine would do something for me. It's Victor, but I never won anything in my life.

Well, on this day me and Brain had been at our house playing computer games on the telly, until my mum got fed up and shooed us out of the house with her squeezy mop. So we went down to my dad's place, under the Arches. That's where the railway viaduct crosses the canal, close to the Town Quay. The arches at the end of the viaduct are over dry land, and they've been blocked in and rented out as workshops. My dad has one of them for his motor-bike repair business, and Brain's dad has another for his joinery. We often go down there if we've nothing else to do.

This particular day we didn't have any choice of which dad to go and see. Brain's dad was away fixing cupboards in somebody's house, and his workshop was locked up. He wouldn't ever let us go there without him, in case we sliced each other up with the circular saw or something. So we both went to *my* dad's. And the first thing we found was that Sam was there before us. She was wearing overalls that belonged to Alan, my dad's mechanic, and she was lying on her back with oil on her face and a spanner in her hand, reckoning to do something to a Yamaha.

Yes, I said 'she'. Sam is a girl. Her full name is Samantha, but she insists on being Sam. Don't call her Samantha, or even Sammy, if you don't want a fight. Sam is our age. She's skinny, but she's tough.

And I was mad, finding her there. I admit, if my dad had asked me to go in and help him I wouldn't have been all that keen. To tell you the truth, I like joinery better than I like motor-bikes. It was just seeing Sam kind of taking my place that annoyed me. Anyway, I made a bit of a fuss, and Sam got up off her back and we shouted at each other and were almost fighting. My dad got fed up and yelled 'Belt up!' at me, and I said, 'Tell *her* to belt up!' and he said, '*Both* of you, belt up!' And Sam said, 'I was all right until *they* came in.' And my dad said, 'Listen! This place isn't big enough to hold you lot *and* me. And I'm staying. And Sam can stay, because she was here first and there wasn't any trouble till you came. So you boys can get out. Go on, off you go!'

Then Sam suddenly changed her tune and said if we had to go she'd go as well. And Dad looked at Sam like she was his blue-eyed girl and said, 'Why not, Sam love? You've helped me a lot already. Why don't you call it a day?'

I knew what he was up to. Sam wanted to go around with

us, and he was on her side. I said we'd nothing to do, and we could do it quite well without Sam.

Dad said, 'God give me strength!'

Brain said, 'Where's Mary-Lou?' Which was a good question. Mary-Lou was Sam's little sister, and most days Sam had to tote her around wherever she went, because their mum was out at work all day.

Sam said, 'Mum's taken her to the dentist's.'

It was then that I noticed this boat, stood up against the wall in a dark corner. Maybe it was a *bit* bigger than a bathtub, but not *much* bigger, and it *looked* like a bathtub.

'How long have you had that?' I asked.

'That thing?' said my dad. 'About a week.'

'How come?' I asked him. 'What did you get it for? Why didn't you *tell* us you had a boat?'

'I took it in part exchange,' my dad said.

Mostly Dad repairs bikes, but sometimes he'll buy and sell them. But it sounded a bit funny.

'A *boat* in exchange for a *bike*?' I said.

'Yes, why not? A lad came in wanting that old Honda that I've had around for ages, but he couldn't raise the deposit. I didn't want to disappoint him. Took the boat as part payment.'

'And what are you going to do with it?'

'Flog it,' said my dad.

'That's mean,' I said. 'You never even asked whether *we'd* have liked a boat.'

'I'm in business,' said Dad. 'And I have to stay in business. It's not so easy these days. That boat's my profit on the deal. Anyway, what do you want a boat for?'

'There's the canal twenty yards away,' I said.

'If you think I'm letting you go boating on this canal,' said my dad, 'you've another think coming.'

'I can swim, can't I?' I said. 'So can Brain.'

'So can I!' said Sam, quick.

'There's waterways that's for pleasure,' said my dad, 'and there's waterways that's for business, just a few of them. But this bit of canal's no good for either business or pleasure. Nobody uses it except that pair of crooks with the scrap-metal boat. The company would close the whole canal down if they could.'

'Gran says canal air's healthy,' I told him. 'She comes down here when she's off-colour and takes a few breaths of it to buck her up.'

'When you're Gran's age,' said Dad, 'you can be as daft as you like, but just for now I don't want you going on that canal. It isn't the air I'm thinking of, it's the water!'

Well, I must admit the canal water wasn't too inviting. It looked black, except when it had a film of oil on it, all rainbow colours. And there was no telling what might flow into it from the pipes behind some of the factories and warehouses along the banks. But I wasn't giving up easily.

'Honestly!' I said. 'Parents! Listen, what's it matter if the water isn't healthy? We're not going to *swim* in it.'

'You might have to. You might fall in.'

'Why should we fall in?' I said. I was getting cross by now.

'Through fooling around,' said my dad. 'Don't try telling me you don't fool around. You and Sam were almost scrapping five minutes ago.'

'We won't fool around in the boat,' I said.

'No, we won't, Mr Horrocks,' said Brain. 'Honest we won't.'

'I don't know what your mums would say,' said Dad.

Well, when he said that, I knew that with just one more push we'd win.

'I *promise* we won't fool around,' I said. 'We'll be dead careful.'

'I promise, too,' said Brain.

'And me,' said Sam.

'Nobody said *you* could come,' I told Sam.

'Listen here, Vic,' said my dad. 'It's my boat, and I lend it to who I like, *if* I like. And if I lend it at all, I'll lend it to the three of you.'

'That's all right,' said Brain. 'We *want* Sam to come.'

I nearly said 'Speak for yourself,' but my dad's eye was on me. There's times when you can argue with my dad and times when you can't. This was one of the times you can't.

Anyway, he gave us all kinds of warnings, including that we were to be back by half past twelve or else, and we weren't to put as much as a little finger in the water, and we were to take fair turns rowing, and we were to watch out when we changed places so as not to upset the boat, and a million billion trillion other things we weren't to do. Above all, we weren't to tell Mum, or *he'd* be in trouble. He went rabbiting on for so long I began to think we'd be due back before he let us go.

In the end Dad helped us carry the boat to the water – it wasn't all that heavy – and steadied it while we got in. There was a pair of plastic oars, and he gave us an old inner tube as a lifebelt. I let Brain have first row, though it meant I had to sit side by side with Sam facing him. Once or twice I glanced over my shoulder and saw that Dad was watching us all the way to the next bridge and out of his sight.

I hadn't been on the canal before. It was quite interesting. The backside of the city, you could call it. Yards with junk in, empty warehouses with all their windows broken, walls of flaking brick with broken glass on top. Then there was a working factory, right on the water's edge, throbbing away, with vapour rising from pipes at the top and liquid swooshing into the canal from pipes lower down. A cindery towpath with nobody on it. Except . . .

Suddenly there was a little kid of six or seven on the towpath ahead of us, jumping up and down and shouting. And we knew her. Oh yes, we knew her all right.

'It's Mary-Lou!' said Sam.

'Take no notice of her,' I said to Brain.

'I'm supposed to look after her,' said Sam.

'I thought you told us she was at the dentist's.'

'Well, she *was*. I expect she's finished now, and my mum's gone to work.'

'We're not taking *her* with us!' I said. 'She's too little.'

'Who are you bossing around?' said Sam, and dug me in the ribs with her elbow. So I pushed her, and she pushed me, and the boat wobbled, and Brain said, 'Stop it, you two. We'd better find out what Mary-Lou wants.'

I knew what Mary-Lou wanted. As soon as we were in reach of the towpath, a body came flying through the air, with about a dozen arms and legs attached to it, or so it seemed. And zonk! Mary-Lou landed in the middle of the boat. And the boat rocked first one way and then the other way, and it looked for a minute as if we were all going overboard. Then the boat righted itself, a bit overloaded, and Mary-Lou sat up in the bottom of it and said, 'Where are we going?'

'We're not going anywhere with *you*!' I said. But Sam said, 'I've *got* to look after her.' Brain said, 'Can she swim?' and Sam said, 'Yes,' and Brain said, 'Oh well, let her come!' And Mary-Lou sat there grinning like a Cheshire cat and said, 'Look at my tooth!' And she pushed her lip back with her finger and showed us the place where it used to be.

'Did the dentist take it out?' asked Sam.

'No. I got in the chair and gave it a good woggle with my tongue, and it came out without him touching it. My mum wasn't half cross. It's in my pocket. Look!' And she started struggling to get at her pocket, and the boat rocked again, and Brain said, 'All right, we believe you,' and Sam said, 'Sit *still*!' and Mary-Lou sat still, more or less, and Brain went on rowing.

We went under two more bridges and past a lot more warehouses and things, and a row of cottages without any roofs on, and then the canal sort of opened out and there were cobbled quays and inlets and mooring-rings and things, and there was an old building that had NORTH-WEST JUNCTION CANAL COMPANY on its side. There wasn't anyone about, and there was barbed wire all over the place and notices saying PRIVATE and KEEP OUT and THIS MEANS YOU, and one that said CAUTION: GUARD DOGS.

'They don't want us to land!' said Brain. Which was pretty obvious.

Mary-Lou asked, 'What do guard dogs do?'

'They chase people and catch them and eat them!' said Brain.

'Ooooh! Would they eat children, too?'

'They love children!' said Brain. 'They have them for dinner every day.'

Mary-Lou put on a frightened look, but you could see she was only pretending.

I reckoned we could get through that barbed wire, and some time when me and Brain were on our own we'd try. But it was no good with Sam and Mary-Lou on board, so I didn't say anything. Brain rowed on a bit, and then we began to hear a kind of swish-swishing noise from ahead of us, and before long we were coming up to where the Urban Throughway crossed the canal.

The swish-swishing was traffic shooting across, and compared with the speed we were going at, the cars seemed to be doing a thousand miles an hour. The canal disappeared into a kind of concrete tunnel under the Throughway, and we rowed into the tunnel, which was small and narrow and seemed to go on and on, the road above it being six lanes wide. We could hear juggernauts and stuff roaring overhead. And at last we came out the other side, and the canal widened out again and was fairly broad.

And on our left was this patch of land. It wasn't an island, but it might as well have been. It was a triangle, with two long sides and a short one. The long sides were the canal that we were on and the railway marshalling yard. The short side was the Throughway, on top of its concrete embankment. It didn't look as if you could get to this patch at all, except by water or by stumbling across about a hundred railway tracks.

'I'm tired of rowing,' said Brain. 'Somebody else have a turn.'

But we were so jam-packed in the little boat, with Mary-Lou still squatting in the middle of it, that we could hardly have managed to change around, and anyway I was getting pins-and-needles, and when Sam said, 'Let's go ashore and explore,' I didn't object, even though it was Sam who said it.

2

Sounds dead easy, doesn't it? 'Let's go ashore and explore.' Well, it wasn't all that easy. The bank was high, and there were reeds and nettles and stuff everywhere, and we were all in this little boat that was weighed right down, and you couldn't move without tipping it sideways. So Brain kind of edged the boat along the bank, and we kept looking for something we could grab hold of, to keep it level while we got out. And there wasn't anything. There just wasn't *anything*.

Then we came to a little inlet. It didn't look much wider than the boat, and there was mud and rushes at each side of it and still nothing we could tie up to. But it was interesting. You could tell that it wasn't there just by accident, it was going somewhere, but you couldn't see *where* it was going because of all the high grass and reeds. So we turned into it. Brain couldn't row any more, because there wasn't enough width for him to use the oars, so me and Sam took an oar each and pushed the boat along by poking at the bottom of the inlet, which was only two or three feet deep.

We were soon out of sight of the main canal or anything else, and it really did feel like an exploration. I expect we only went twenty or thirty yards along the inlet, but it felt like a lot more. Then the way was blocked by a massive beam of wood, lying straight across the water but half out of it, and resting on supports at each side of the inlet. You could see that the inlet had been seven or eight feet wide before it got all silted up.

We didn't mind the beam being there, because we were able

to edge the boat up to it, and Brain held on to one of the supports, and I got out on to the beam, and in a minute or two we were all ashore and the boat was tied up, although even that wasn't as easy as it sounds, and Mary-Lou teetered along the beam as if she was going to fall in any minute, and she wouldn't have come up smelling of roses and violets if she had.

And then we saw that, further up the inlet beyond the beam, there was something in the water, blocking the way completely. Something black and bulky. It was the tarred hull of a canal cargo-boat. It was tethered with a huge rusty chain, which by now was pointless, because that boat was well and truly stuck in the mud, and wasn't ever going to go anywhere again. But the chain was so big and stout it looked as if it would last for ever, and it must have lasted a good many years already.

The ground was fairly firm alongside the boat, so we could get close to it and peer over the edge, and you could see that it wasn't much more than a carcass, with timbers like ribs sticking up and the front three-quarters of it all full of water. There were a few cross-beams here and there, and a couple of big thick heavy planks laid across the middle of them, lengthways along the boat, and at the back end there were the remains of a cabin, with a bit of rusty chimney sticking up out of the roof and sagging walls that were coming unstuck from the corner-posts.

Well, of course, we wanted to take a good look at it. Wouldn't you? Me and Brain climbed up on to the sides of the hull, and there was a sort of catwalk running all the way round, that was very narrow but you were all right as long as you could keep your footing and not fall into the water inside. There must have been lots of mud in the hull, because there were weeds and a little tree that had planted themselves and were doing fine. We couldn't get into the cabin, because the door to it opened from the back deck, and the back deck wasn't there any more. We could see that the floorboards of the cabin had rotted away, too.

Meanwhile there was Mary-Lou on the shore yelling that she wanted to come too, and Sam holding her back and getting mad because she couldn't come up without letting go of Mary-Lou. Anyway, Brain went and held Mary-Lou for a bit and lifted her on to his shoulders so that she could see into the boat from the bank, and Sam climbed up on the catwalk and went trotting over the planks and crawling and jumping on places where I wouldn't have risked it, but Sam is so light and skinny she could get away with it.

I expect you can guess what we were all thinking. We were thinking just what *you'd* have been thinking if it had been you. We were reckoning we could repair that cabin and make a den out of it.

Sam went back and took another turn at holding Mary-Lou, which was getting to be difficult, the way she was kicking and carrying on and wanting some of the action. Me and Brain tried to move one of the planks from the front end so as to

make a way to the cabin, but it was thick and heavy and slimy and we couldn't shift it. Then suddenly Brain said, 'What time is it?' and Sam looked at her watch and said it was after twelve, and we knew we'd be late back. So we gave up and piled back into our own boat and edged it down to the canal again, and this time it was me that was rowing. Me and Brain were all muddy, but Sam in some mysterious way had managed not to get dirty at all, though she'd been into everything just the same as we had.

All the way back to the Arches we talked about what we could do with that cabin. Mary-Lou had as much to say as anyone else. She wanted it made into a Wendy-house. Some hope. The rest of us thought it should be a gang headquarters. I reckoned Mary-Lou should be kept out of all this, because she'd either get drowned or drive us crazy, but Sam said that with her mum being at work she just had to take Mary-Lou everywhere. And Brain said that Sam had found the boat

along with us, and she had a right to be in the gang, and if Sam wasn't in it there wasn't going to *be* any gang, and if that meant having Mary-Lou as well we'd have to have Mary-Lou as well. Which made me cross, seeing that Brain's supposed to be *my* pal. Anyway, Sam and Mary-Lou insisted that Mary-Lou was a good swimmer, so we decided we'd have to let her come and just keep an eye on her, especially Sam.

We got back to the Arches a quarter of an hour late. My dad didn't fuss about that. He said he'd expected us to be a *bit* late, but if we'd been a *lot* late there'd have been trouble. He let us wash at the sink behind his workshop, and lent us a scrubbing-brush to get some of the muck off our clothes. We were wearing old things anyway, and Dad reckoned Brain's dad wouldn't notice but my mum might have something to say.

'Where have you been,' Dad asked us, 'to get into that state?'

So we started to tell him.

'Don't all talk at once,' he said, though me and Brain and Sam weren't all talking at once, it was Mary-Lou who was all talking at once, enough for half a dozen. Anyway, Sam shut her up and we explained that we'd been to this plot of land that was cut off by the Throughway. I reckoned my dad would know all about it, because he's lived here all his life, and he can tell you more about Claypits than you'd ever want to know, and if you give him half a chance he *will*.

'I remember that patch,' he said. 'It used to be bigger. There was a house and stabling and a landing-stage on it, but they all had to go, to make room for the Throughway. So there's nothing now but the remaining bit of land. I don't know who owns it, but whoever it is, it's no use to him. You couldn't build or do anything with that patch. No access.'

Then my dad got that faraway look in his eye that means he's thinking back to when he was a lad and before you know where you are he'll be telling you all about it, so if you don't want my dad's memoirs you'd better get out of the way, quick. But this time we were interested, so we stayed around.

'We used to play there,' he said, 'when I was your age. You could get to it easily in those days, before the Throughway. We called it Tom Tiddler's Ground. But we never found any gold or silver.'

Me and Brain and Sam all stared at him.

'Gold and silver?' I said. 'What are you talking about?'

'Here we come on Tom Tiddler's Ground,' said my dad in a chanting kind of voice. 'Picking up gold and silver.'

Well, we'd never heard of Tom Tiddler's Ground. I bet *you* haven't, either. We know now, because my dad told us.

'Tom Tiddler's Ground is a game,' he said. 'Or was, in my young days. You chalk a line on the playground, or scratch it in the gravel or whatever, and one side of the line is Tom Tiddler's Ground. One of you is Tom Tiddler. The other kids trespass across the line, pretending to pick up gold and silver, and Tom Tiddler chases them and tries to catch one. But he's not allowed to go their side of the line. And while he's chasing one lot of kids at one end, a different lot will start crossing the line at the other end.'

'And what happens when he catches one?'

'The one that's caught becomes Tom Tiddler,' said my dad. 'Mind you, it was an old-fashioned game, even in my day. I don't suppose it's ever played now. I'd forgotten it myself, till you mentioned that bit of land.'

'So we've been on Tom Tiddler's Ground!' I said. It sounded good.

Mary-Lou started chanting, the way my dad had done, in her little kid's voice:

> 'Here we come on Tom Tiddler's Ground,
>   Picking up gold and sil-ver!'

and then, repeating herself over and over again:

'Picking up gold and sil-ver,
Picking up gold and sil-ver,
Picking up gold and sil-ver!'

'I'll gold-and-silver *you* in a minute!' said Sam, which made Mary-Lou giggle.

I told my dad we were thinking of making a den, because my dad is the kind of grown-up who understands that kids like making dens. My mum says he's a kid of forty-three himself. I didn't tell him about the canal-boat, though. I had a kind of instinct that he wouldn't want us to tamper with that, I don't know why. As it was, he just said, 'Well, if you make a den on that plot you'll be trespassing. I can't see anyone worrying about it, but don't come complaining to me if you get thrown out, that's all I have to say. And now, young Vic, you'd best be getting home for your dinner!'

My dad takes sandwiches, because he doesn't close the workshop at dinner-time, but I go home for dinner in the school holidays.

'And I hope you've got a good story ready for your mum,' Dad said, 'because you're still a bit of a sight.'

'Me and Sam aren't a sight,' said Mary-Lou virtuously. 'Me and Sam are *clean*!' And off she went, holding Sam's hand and chanting again:

'Picking up gold and sil-ver,
Picking up gold and sil-ver,
Picking up gold and sil-ver!

Go on, gold-and-silver *me*, Sam. I'd like to be gold and silver!'

3

There was trouble all right when I got home, but it wasn't Mum, it was Gran. My mum may grouse a bit, but she doesn't mind all *that* much if I get a bit mucky. 'Lads are *like* that,' she says.

But our gran, oh, she's a Tartar. She lives three doors away, and she's in and out of our house all the time. She's my dad's mother, and she doesn't approve of Mum. She reckons Mum doesn't look after Dad properly. That's because Mum isn't always running around after him. Also, Gran reckons Mum doesn't bring me up as strictly as she ought.

'If *I'd* behaved like that, my dad would have given me the strap,' is the kind of thing she says to Mum about me.

A funny thing about Gran is that she never speaks to me directly. She speaks to Mum or Dad *about* me, with me standing there listening. Like she did on this particular day, when she began by saying to Mum, 'Just *look* at him! I never *saw* a child in such a state!'

My mum looked at me and sighed and shook her head and said, 'Oh, Vïc, what *are* we going to do with you?'

Gran said, 'I know what *I'd* do with him. When Bill and Sidney' (that's my dad and Uncle Sid) 'were his age, if they'd come in like that, they'd have got a good hiding and been sent to bed.'

Mum said, 'What happened, Vic?'

I said, 'Nothing.'

'What were you doing?'

'Playing.'

Gran said, 'He doesn't even give his mother a proper answer.'

I said, 'If you want to know, we're making a den. Me and Brain and Sam.'

Mum said, 'It must be a mud hut you're making. It's a good job you're in your old clothes.'

Gran said, 'Old clothes? When I was a child, we'd have been glad of clothes like that for our Sunday best. And we wouldn't have treated them the way *he* does, or my dad would have taken the strap to us!'

Mum said, 'Yes, well, times have changed.'

Gran said, snorting, 'You don't have to tell me that. Children aren't brought up the way they used to be. And look at the result. All these vandals and football hooligans. Don't blame *me* if Victor turns out badly.'

'Oh, for heaven's sake,' said Mum, dishing up the meal, 'it's nothing but a bit of dirt. It'll brush off all right when it's dry.'

So then Gran bristled and said, 'That's right, stand up for him against me! I suppose I should expect it. You've always had your own ideas, haven't you? Well, Brenda, all I can say is, they're not mine!'

Mum snapped back at her, just as cross, 'I know. And I don't look after your son the way I should. I ought to wait on him hand and foot, oughtn't I?'

Then they were off. They have these rows from time to time. Mum and Dad thought they were going to get a bit of peace when Gran went into the Sheltered Housing, out at Scarsholme. You should have seen their faces when we visited her there and Gran said she didn't like it and was coming back to her old house in Claypits. Dad is pretty patient with Gran – well, after all, she *is* his mother – but Mum sees much more of her than Dad does, and sometimes Gran drives her bananas.

Anyway, before long they were going at it hammer and

tongs. I ate up my dinner and said, 'I'm off out again, back at teatime,' and they were so busy they hardly noticed I was going. I went down to the Arches, and found that Brain's dad was back in his workshop and Brain and Sam were begging wood and stuff from him, in between trying to keep tabs on Mary-Lou, who was into everything as usual.

'I ought to *insure* against having that child around,' Brain's dad said. 'I'd better give you something to get rid of you all.' He's a helpful sort of fellow, and he gave us some offcuts and odd lengths of timber and some nails, and even lent us some tools, though I reckon they were about his tenth best.

There was a problem, which was that although you could get to Tom Tiddler's Ground by water, the little plastic boat wasn't going to hold four of us and the timber as well. Seemed to me the answer was to leave some of us behind, especially Mary-Lou. We got all heated about that. Sam said we couldn't just leave Mary-Lou and we needn't think we were going to leave both of them and go off having all the fun without them. Brain sided with Sam. In the end it was Brain who came up with an answer, which was for one of us to row the boat with all the stuff, and unload it at the inlet, and then row a little way back as far as the canal basin, while the other three made their way to the canal basin by land and were picked up there. They'd have to get through the barbed wire somehow. Brain reckoned they could make it.

Well, that seemed to be the best we could do. Somebody had to be Joe Soap and row a boatload of stuff all on his own, and finish up all aches and blisters. Guess who it was. You're right. It was Muggins here. I did the rowing, and was it hot, and did it seem a long way to go without any company! I'm not asking you, I'm telling you. And it was a struggle to unload the stuff when I got there. I was all cross and sweaty by the time I'd rowed the half-mile back under the Throughway and up to the canal basin.

And there they were, Brain and Sam and Mary-Lou, sitting in a row on the edge of a quay, looking as cool as cucumbers. They'd found a place where they could squeeze through the barbed wire without anything happening except Brain getting a tear in the seat of his pants, but it was only a little one and he reckoned his dad would never notice. And they'd got a can of Pepsi, and I must admit they'd saved some for me, but it was only enough to make me thirstier.

Brain started telling me the way they'd come, through all the back streets and alleys. It sounded just like my dad telling some other fellow about the best route for driving from somewhere to somewhere else, which is the most boring kind of conversation I know. I told Brain to wrap up and get in the boat. And right at that moment I saw someone wriggling under the barbed wire to come to join us.

I said a rude word that made Mary-Lou go round-eyed and say 'Ooooh!' Well, I had a right to. Of all the kids in the world, it was just about the one I least wanted to see. It was Darryl Tooke.

Is there a kid in your school that wants to be everybody's pal but that nobody wants to be the pal of? There is in ours, and it's Darryl. He comes up to you, and if he was a dog he'd be trying to lick your face but expecting to get kicked. And I dare say if he was a dog he'd be liked better. If you encourage him at all, he hooks on to you and you can't get rid of him. I'm sorry for Darryl in a way. He's really poor and lives in a kind of attic flat with his mum, and they say his mum is up to no good. I wouldn't know about that. Darryl never has to go in for meals or bedtimes or anything, and nobody cares what state his clothes are in. Other kids' parents don't actually say anything, but they don't like it if their children play with Darryl.

'Where you going in that boat?' he asked us.

'Nowhere.'

'Can I come?'

'No.'

'You can *see* there's no room for anybody else,' said Brain in a reasonable tone of voice. 'If anyone else got in, it'd *sink*.'

Darryl laughed in a flattering way, as if Brain had said something clever.

'Let's go,' I said. 'At least he can't follow us where *we're* going.'

I was wrong, though. Darryl *could* follow us. How do you suppose he did it? Yes, that's right, you've guessed. He was wearing a ragged T-shirt and old jeans torn off at the knees, and just as we rowed away from the quay there was a splash and Darryl dived into the canal fully dressed, if you can call it fully dressed. He came to the surface about twelve feet from where he went in, and came swimming after us in a real expert crawl, like a fish, except I don't suppose fishes swim the crawl. I don't know how a kid like Darryl learned to swim like that. He was faster than we were. If he'd caught hold of the boat he'd probably have tipped us all in, whether he meant to or not, so I fended him off with an oar, and that made us wobble enough to give us a fright. Darryl kept his distance and swam alongside.

I said, 'I told you, you're not coming.'

Brain said, 'He *is* coming. We can't stop him.'

Sam said, '*He* doesn't seem to mind the canal water.'

Brain said, 'Darryl doesn't mind anything.'

Darryl just swam. At least he had his mouth closed.

I didn't really fancy Darryl finding out where we were going, but there was nothing much we could do about it except cross the canal to the towpath and wait around until Darryl got tired and went away, and if I knew Darryl he might hang around for hours. So I just rowed straight on, under the Throughway, and tied the boat up beside the beam where we'd left it before, and we all got out on to Tom Tiddler's Ground. And Darryl climbed out of the water and shook

himself like a dog and came up to us, grinning all over his face but looking a bit wary all the same, ready to take himself out of range, quick, if he needed to.

'It's bad enough,' I said, 'having Mary-Lou. We're not having him as well.'

Then Sam had this bright idea. I admit it was a bright idea. I've never said Sam was *slow*.

'You can stay with us if you like, Darryl,' she said, 'but you have to look after Mary-Lou, right?'

I don't think any boy but Darryl would have agreed to that. But I reckon Darryl wanted to be with us at any price. He nodded and grinned and said, 'All right, Sam.' And you'll hardly believe it, but Mary-Lou said, 'Yes, I want Darryl to look after me,' and went up to him and held his hand and looked at him as if he was the greatest. And Darryl didn't seem to mind and didn't even pull his hand away, but stood there looking as if he'd won a prize. You'd think he actually *wanted* a kid sister.

So that made five of us. I'd rather it had been just Brain and me, though I was getting used to Sam by now. We were stuck with Darryl and Mary-Lou, and it looked as if we had them for keeps. Five is a gang, and if you ask me, a gang needs a boss. I said so, and told them I thought I should be it.

There was no end of fuss over that. Sam said she wasn't going to be bossed by me or anybody else. Brain said if we had a boss at all it should be Sam. I said I wasn't having a girl as boss. Mary-Lou suggested Darryl, but we all squashed that idea, seeing Darryl had only just joined, and anyway Darryl is so skinny and scruffy that nobody would ever make him boss of anything. Darryl said the boss should be me or Brain or maybe Sam. It all got so confused we didn't know whether we were coming or going. In the end we decided that Brain and Sam and me should be joint bosses and the other two should be ordinary members. Seemed to me that wasn't much better than not having a boss at all.

We swore the ordinary members to secrecy, and then we showed Darryl the canal-boat. He said he'd seen it before, but we took no notice of that. We picked up the timber that I'd dumped and carted it along to the boat, and we started to work out how we'd do the repair job.

4

Do you want to know how we repaired that cabin? Well, you needn't think I'm going to spell it all out a nail at a time. It was bad enough doing the job, without having to explain it to somebody afterwards.

I'll tell you a *bit* about it, though. We fixed the sides with marine plywood and the roof with roofing-felt and the floor with chipboard, the heavy sort. I dare say that sounds simple to you. Well, it wasn't. It took just over a week, working hard every day, and I reckon that was good going. First there was a lot of measuring up and getting more stuff there, and it was a long way back if you found you'd forgotten something. Then the hull was full of water, and although the cabin itself was above water-level we had to arrange a system of planks to stand on while we worked, and we had to watch out all the time not to step back and not to drop any tools. And everything had to be done by hand. It was no good borrowing an electric saw or drill from Brain's dad, because there wasn't a power-point in miles. In some places the wood of the boat was so hard it bent the nails, and in other parts it was so soft and rotten it wouldn't hold them. I guess we learned a bit about carpentry while we were doing it. Enough to last me a lifetime, I sometimes thought.

The weather was hot all the time, which was good in a way, because me and Brain could work in our swimming trunks (it didn't matter to Darryl, who wore the same old rubbish clothes whatever he did, and didn't care how wet or dirty he got). But

31

in another way it wasn't so good, because we got all sweaty and bad-tempered, and shouted at each other.

And then there was Mary-Lou. I must admit, Darryl did his best to keep her happy and quiet and out from under our feet, but it wasn't in Mary-Lou's nature not to be in the midst of anything that was going on. Sam ticked her off about every two minutes for this or that, but got all steamed up if anyone else tried to do it, so there was a bit of trouble over that. And Mary-Lou drove us all up the wall with not being able to stop chanting about Tom Tiddler's Ground and gold and silver. She'd sing that second line over and over again – 'Picking up gold and *sil*-ver, picking up gold and *sil*-ver' – until I felt I wanted to drown her, although I reckon you *couldn't* drown Mary-Lou. If you'd dropped her in the canal in a sack tied up at the neck and loaded with stones, you'd only have had to turn your back and she'd have been sitting on the bank again, chanting, 'Picking up gold and *sil*-ver!'

The funny thing is, it was Mary-Lou who *did* find something, and although it wasn't exactly gold and silver, it was something of the sort, in a small way. It was a day when she was making a nuisance of herself, going on and on about wanting to help. If there was one thing worse than Mary-Lou hindering you, it was Mary-Lou trying to help. Anyway, we'd set her to work pulling up weeds and stuff that had rooted themselves in crannies in the hull where soil had lodged. Darryl was watching over her, as he'd promised, and having quite a job keeping hold of her while she leaned and teetered and did tight-rope acts all over the place. And suddenly, late in the afternoon when we were just about to go home, Mary-Lou squeaked, 'I've found something!'

We didn't take any notice. Mary-Lou was finding things all the time, and they were usually half-bricks or lumps of wood. She only went on about them because she was always going on about *something*, trying to get attention.

Then she yelled, 'It's stuck!', whatever it was. And we still didn't take any notice. She was groping about in the rear of the hull, under where the back deck had been, and she had her arm in the water nearly up to the shoulder. She called to Darryl to help her, and leaned over still further with Darryl holding her round the middle, and if he'd let go she'd have fallen into the bilgewater. And at last we all took an interest. A moment later Mary-Lou let out a shriek of triumph and pulled her arm from the water, and she was holding a glass jar with a screw-top still in place, and it had round black things in it, and we could see at once that they were coins.

Darryl dragged Mary-Lou to safety on dry land and we all gathered round. At first we couldn't get the lid off the jar. We all had a go at shifting it, but it wouldn't budge. Then I had a second go, and I used all my strength until I could feel myself getting red in the face with the effort, and then, wow! off it came, and I felt pretty good. And we tipped the coins out on the grass.

There were about twenty of them. They had pictures of men's or ladies' heads on them, and words in Latin. I've written down the words that were on the biggest number of coins. They said GEORGIUS V DEI GRA BRITT OMN REX FID DEF IND IMP. I thought they were probably Roman, and maybe we would get a reward for finding them. But Brain said, 'Don't you know what those are? They're old pennies.'

I'd never seen an old penny before. They were much bigger than modern ones. I asked if they were valuable, and Brain said he didn't think they were, and Sam said they didn't belong to us, which was just the kind of awkward thing she *would* think of. Mary-Lou said *she* had found them, and it was finders keepers. We couldn't make up our minds what to do about them, and seeing it was time to go home we put them back in the jar for the time being and hid it under a great big tangled bramble-bush that was near the old boat.

We argued about the pennies all the way back to the Arches and all the way to Tom Tiddler's Ground again next morning. In the end we decided there was no way of telling who they really belonged to, and probably whoever it was had died years ago. Brain said in that case the coins were Treasure Trove, and if we reported them we'd have to explain where we'd found them, and then we might be told to stop working on the cabin. We didn't want that. But then Brain thought of something else. His dad had told him that when the new pennies came in, about fifteen years ago, one new penny was worth two and a half old pennies.

'So twenty old pennies would only be worth 8p,' he said.

Well, even Sam agreed that 8p wasn't much of a Treasure Trove, and that we didn't have to worry all that much about who owned it.

'Can we *spend* the pennies?' asked Mary-Lou.

'No,' said Brain. 'They won't take them in the shops.'

'Tell you what, though,' said Sam. 'We could use them in the Penny Machine Museum.'

'Ooh, yes!' squealed Mary-Lou, jumping up and down.

I'd never heard of the Penny Machine Museum. Sam and Mary-Lou knew about it because their mum had taken them there the year before. It was in the city centre, in a little street near the Central Library. There were all sorts of funny machines that were worked by putting one of these old pennies in the slot. The people in the museum charged you two new pence for one old penny to put in the slot, and then they got the old penny back when the machine was emptied. It sounded like good business to me. But if you'd got your own old pennies, you wouldn't need to buy them.

We'd been working on that cabin all week, and we were due for a break. So after dinner we went to the Penny Machine Museum instead. And it was great. There were machines that were glass cases with battles and things going on in them that you could set moving by putting your penny in, and there was one I specially liked, which was the Execution of King Charles the First, and they brought this king out and laid him down and there was a fellow with an axe that went zonk! and the king's head flew off. You could see that the head was on wires, but it was good all the same. There were kind of long-ago juke-boxes that played plinkety-plonk tunes when you put a penny in. And there was one called 'What the Butler Saw', where you put your eye to a pretend keyhole and there was a lady un-dressing wearing enormous knickers. Darryl said there were more interesting ladies on Page 3 of the *Sun* every day, and Brain said yes, but they didn't have knickers like that, and Sam said boys were disgusting.

The lady at the counter came and asked us about our money, because we hadn't bought any pennies from her. We told her we'd found it by the canal, which was just about true, and she was all right and didn't mind. She said they were glad to have old pennies brought in, because they lost quite a few through people buying them and then keeping them instead of putting them in the machines. So we used ours all up and saw all the machines working except one or two that looked dull, and we had King Charles the First executed three times over.

The next day we really got on with our work on the boat, all except Mary-Lou, who thought she would find some more money and hunted all over the place, chanting about gold and silver, but she didn't find anything. We got the cabin floor fixed, and it was as solid as anything. It poured with rain that night, but when we went along next day the cabin was quite dry. We'd put new hinges on the door, and Brain had got hold of a padlock and chain, so we reckoned we could safely keep things there.

We'd just about finished by now. We put some shelves up, and Mum gave me a couple of folding benches and an old card-table that were in the roof-space at home, and Sam got some cups and plates and a bit of carpet, and Brain's dad lent us a Primus stove, so we were really set up. It was the best den any of us had ever had, and I bet you've never had one like it.

Working on it had made us into good friends, even Sam and me, because I must admit Sam had done her share, and it wasn't her fault she had to tote Mary-Lou around with her, and anyway Darryl was doing most of the looking after Mary-Lou and didn't seem to mind. We had our headquarters now, and we reckoned that when it was fine we could go exploring with the little plastic boat, and when it was wet we'd stay in the cabin and play games. We brought some of our favourite things along. Brain brought his Monopoly set and his electronic chess that his dad had given him for his birthday. I brought my radio and Sam brought a row of glass animals to stand on the shelf and Mary-Lou brought a teddy-bear with only one eye called Nelson. Darryl didn't bring anything, because Darryl doesn't have anything to bring.

You may think we were daft to keep expensive things like a radio and an electronic chess-game in the cabin of an old canal-boat on a patch of waste land. Yes, well, I think so myself now. But remember it was locked, and all the time we'd been working on the boat nobody had bothered us or even come near the place. Seeing it was so hard to get to, there didn't seem any reason why anybody ever should.

So it was a shock when, a few days later, we got there in the morning and found there'd been intruders.

5

It was horrible. The day was bright, and we'd brought some bottles of pop, and all the way from the Arches to Tom Tiddler's Ground we'd been planning what we were going to do that morning. We meant to explore further along the canal towards the East Basin, which was as far as you could get in this direction, because beyond that point it had been filled in. Brain had a big sheet of cartridge paper and some coloured pencils, and we were going to make a map showing where we'd been.

But first we wanted to go to the cabin and pick up a jumper that Sam had left there and just gloat a bit over the cabin being such a terrific place and all our own work. So we tied the little boat to the beam as we'd done before and got out and walked up to the canal-boat, and the first thing we saw was that the padlock and hasp had been wrenched off and the door was hanging open. And if it's never happened to you, you can't guess what a sickening feeling it gives you to see a thing like that.

Brain and me broke into a run and charged up the plank into the back of the boat. We didn't stop to think whether the people who'd broken in might still be there, but they weren't. Still, they'd been there quite a while. There were half a dozen empty beer-bottles around, and a stink of beer and cigarette-smoke, and fag-ends had been dropped on the carpet. And that wasn't all. My radio had gone. So had Brain's electronic chess-game. Sam's glass animals had been thrown down and trodden on and were nearly all broken. Her jumper was on the floor with a muddy boot-print on it. The only thing that hadn't been touched was poor old Nelson, Mary-Lou's teddy-bear, who was so decrepit you couldn't do him much harm.

I felt weak in my legs and at the same time sick in my stomach. Brain, who hardly ever swears, said some terrible words. I've never seen Sam cry, but I reckon she was close to it that morning. She went down on her knees picking up her broken animals, very carefully. There was just one that wasn't damaged, a deer or something, and she rescued it and put it back on the shelf it had fallen off. And Mary-Lou picked up Nelson and cuddled him and seemed to think he must have suffered from seeing all this going on around him.

'Well,' I said, 'what do we do now?'

Just at that moment, I'd have liked to turn my back on the whole thing and go away and never come near the place again for the rest of my life. It was as bad as that. Everything seemed ruined. It wasn't just the theft and damage, it was the rottenness of it, to think that people would *do* such a thing. And besides, if we did put the cabin to rights, it was likely to be broken into again.

I think Brain and Sam felt the same way at first.

'We'll have to tell our dads,' said Brain. 'I mean, anyway, mine'd want to know what happened to the chess-set.'

'And mine'd want to know about the radio,' said I.

Sam reckoned she could get away without telling her mum, so long as she could stop Mary-Lou talking. They were going on a week's holiday next day, and her mum's mind was full of that.

We had a good look all over the site, just in case the missing things had been left around or there was some clue as to who had taken them, but we didn't find anything, and we set off back along the canal the way we'd come, feeling very woe-begone.

And telling our parents wasn't any fun at all. Brain's dad was really cross about the chess, which had cost a lot of money. He said Brain had no sense at all, and he needn't think he was going to get another one in place of it because he wasn't, and a lot more besides. My dad was a bit more sympathetic than Brain's, but even so he said I deserved to lose the radio. He asked if I had any idea who the thieves might be. We had all talked about this on the way back to the Arches and had wondered if it could be Ken and Morry Aston, a pair of big lads who were always in trouble, but when I mentioned them to Dad he said right away that the Astons were on holiday on the Costa Brava, so it couldn't be them. I didn't have any other ideas. Dad said we wouldn't get anywhere by telling the police, because we hadn't any right to be on that boat anyway.

'It's a hard world, son,' he said, 'and there's some lessons that have to be learned the hard way. If I was you, I wouldn't go to that place again. Don't say too much to your mum, because she'll think *you* might have been bashed up, not just your den. Don't say anything at all to your gran. And listen, Vic, why don't you all go to the baths this afternoon, for a change? I'll give you the money.'

He pulled a face when he found there were five of us, but he paid for us all. I had to lend Darryl my old swimming trunks, because he didn't have any such thing and they won't let you swim in your underpants or in torn-off jeans. Still, it was a good idea of my dad's, and it did take our minds off the disaster.

Next morning, when I met Brain, we were in a mood to fight back. Sam had gone away on holiday now, but we knew she'd think as we did. It was *our* den, and we weren't going to give it up at the first sign of trouble. After we'd talked it over a bit, Brain said, 'I know what we'll do. We'll set a booby-trap in case they come again.'

I thought that was a terrific idea. Next day we went to the

canal-boat for the first time in three days. There was no sign that anyone had been there in the meantime. And we booby-trapped it three ways. We set the gangplank with its upper end on the very edge of the boat, so that if anybody stepped on it it would slip and he'd fall into the water, or so we hoped. We took up a piece of the chipboard floor just inside the cabin door and replaced the carpet over it, so that anyone who did get in would fall through the hole. And when we locked the cabin up before leaving it, we smeared the padlock and chain with some tar that Brain had scooped up from the roadworks near his house. It cheered us up a lot to do this. We kept picturing the intruders arriving and having a chapter of accidents. We almost *hoped* they'd come back, and were sorry that we wouldn't see the fun.

While Sam and Mary-Lou were away, me and Brain and Darryl fooled around together and had quite a good time, and we went every day to the canal-boat to see what had happened. But nothing happened at all. Each time we went, we had to put the gangplank back so that it didn't slip, and we had to try not to get tar on our own hands. Each time we got into the cabin we found the carpet still in place over the gap, and obviously no one had been near. And it's funny how soon, when nothing happens for a while, you get to think that nothing ever *will*.

By the end of the week we'd put the piece of floor back, because it was such a pain having to step round it all the time. We'd wiped off the tar, which was getting on our faces and clothes and everything. And we'd stopped booby-trapping the gangplank, because the only person who'd been caught by the booby-trap was Darryl. He forgot it was there, and it worked a treat and dropped him in mucky water up to his waist. It would have ruined his clothes if they hadn't been past ruin already.

When Sam came back from holiday, we told her nobody but

us had been to the den. And within a day or two we were using it just as if nothing had ever happened, the only difference being that we didn't leave anything valuable there.

Mary-Lou had come back bursting with energy and wanting to go fishing around in the hull for more treasure. Sam didn't like her doing that, but had a bright idea for keeping her busy. She started making a garden around the landward end of the gangplank, and got Mary-Lou to bring her toy spade and share the digging.

'You're more likely to find treasure on land than in an old boat,' Sam told Mary-Lou. 'Most treasure is *buried*. If you help me dig, you might find some.'

That was all right for a while, but Mary-Lou wanted results. She dug away like mad at first, but when she didn't find anything she began to lose interest, and by the end of the day she was all eagerness to get back to the boat and see what might still be under all that water. Then Sam had a second bright idea.

'Let's bury something for her to find,' she said to Brain and me.

We both looked around at home for something that would serve as buried treasure, and Brain came up with the best thing, which was a silver teaspoon with an enamelled badge at the end of the stem saying CITY OF MELBOURNE CENTENARY 1935. It was small and easy to bury, and Mary-Lou would be thrilled with it.

Next morning Sam kept Mary-Lou busy with something else for a few minutes while me and Brain buried the spoon. Mary-Lou wasn't all that keen to start digging after she hadn't found anything yesterday, but we all gathered round and encouraged her and told her she was bound to find something before long. And we thought for a while she was somehow going to miss finding the spoon, but in the end her spade clinked on it and out it came.

It worked a treat. Mary-Lou didn't suspect a thing. She danced around, waving the spoon in the air.

'It's silver!' she yelled. 'I'm picking up gold and silver!'

We had a long argument about how a silver spoon could have found its way here from the other side of the world. Sam said maybe the canal-boat had been to Australia. Brain said canal-boats couldn't cross the ocean, and probably the spoon had been lost in the sand over there and had worked its way through the earth and come out our side. He said this with a straight face, and I think Darryl would have believed it if he hadn't actually seen the spoon buried, but Mary-Lou told Brain not to be silly.

Anyway, this set Mary-Lou digging with even more energy, and for the rest of the day she went at it non-stop, giving us a bit of peace, apart from the chanting about being on Tom Tiddler's Ground picking up gold and *sil*-ver.

'How are we going to keep her going?' said Sam. 'She'll expect to find something else before long.'

Actually it was worse than just expecting to find something else. Mary-Lou was getting big ideas. She'd found copper coins and a silver spoon, and she told us that next time it would be *gold* she found. I think she really believed it. We didn't see how we could provide her with gold. I remembered an old brass door-knob that my dad had taken off the kitchen door and replaced with plastic. I thought it might look like gold if we rubbed it up with metal-polish, but Brain reckoned that even Mary-Lou wouldn't be taken in by an old door-knob.

That was the day when Brain and Sam and me started playing Monopoly. Have you played it? It goes on for ever. Me and Sam hadn't played before, and we weren't all that keen at first, but Brain showed us, and we got hooked. Before long we were buying and selling property and charging each other rent and squabbling a bit, and we could hardly manage to break off when it was time to go home.

Next morning we were at it again. Darryl didn't want to play, but we didn't mind that. We left him to look after Mary-Lou while we went on with the game. And when we finished the first game we started another right away. And what with throwing the dice and doing deals and counting Monopoly money and all watching each other like hawks, we weren't thinking of anything else at all.

Then we heard a splash, and Darryl's voice yelling 'Sam! Sam!' We dropped everything, dashed from the cabin and edged our way as fast as we could round the catwalk. There was Darryl, lying face-down along a plank over the water that filled the hold of the boat, and gripping Mary-Lou by the shoulder of her T-shirt. Mary-Lou's face was above water. She was coughing and spluttering, and water was streaming from her hair.

You should have seen Sam. Straight into the water with a jump. Standing up in it (it was only up to her waist) and wrapping her arms round Mary-Lou's midriff. Passing her up to us. And there was Brain and me and Darryl all trying to take hold of her and getting tangled up together and almost falling into the water in a bunch. A proper shambles, but somehow finishing up with all of us safe and sound on the bank and Mary-Lou flat on her tummy drawing great sobbing breaths. Sam shouting at Darryl, 'What d'you let her do *that* for?' and Darryl answering, all miserable, 'I couldn't stop her.' And Sam, suddenly, 'What's she got in her hand?' And Mary-Lou, recovering like magic, her voice still choky but triumphant, 'Look! I got it! *Gold!*'

She was holding up a flat, gold-looking disc, about three inches across. There was a pattern on it. An eye, surrounded by marks that looked like the sun's rays, and a border round the edge, and a kind of metal loop.

'Gold!' proclaimed Mary-Lou again.

We all peered at the thing. It was Brain who decided what it was.

'It's a horse-brass!' he said. 'You know, things horses used to wear on their harness.'

'Gold!' said Mary-Lou again.

'No, not gold. Brass. They sell them at the gift shop in Hibiscus Street.'

'Not valuable?' I asked.

'No. Ten a penny.'

'Not worth getting wet through for,' said Sam crossly, 'never mind being nearly drowned!'

'She wouldn't have got drowned,' said Brain. 'It was just a fright, that's all.'

'Well, it was bad enough,' said Sam. 'Now we'd better go home.'

But they didn't go home. It was blazing hot, and Sam and Mary-Lou were only wearing T-shirts and shorts and plastic sandals, and their clothes soon dried on them and were none the worse. Mary-Lou was over the moon, because she still thought she'd struck gold and she wouldn't listen to what the rest of us said. I must admit, that kid was the world's number-one finder. She said she'd spotted the edge of the horse-brass in the mud in the bottom of the boat and she was poking at it with a long stick when she fell in. We let her stand it in the middle of the shelf, where it looked a bit weird with its one eye staring out into the cabin.

'I've never seen one like that before,' said Brain.

'P'raps it's a *real* horse-brass,' suggested Sam. 'Maybe it came off a horse's harness, not out of a shop. They had horses to pull the barges in the old days, didn't they?'

Brain said they did, but he still didn't think it was worth much. Mary-Lou insisted it was hers, but she and Sam didn't want to take it home because they didn't want to tell their mum how they'd got it. In the end we left it there on the shelf, which we wouldn't have done if we'd thought it was valuable.

All the way home, and again during the evening watching

telly, I kept thinking about that horse-brass. There was something funny about it. Something wrong. Maybe you've seen what it was. It seems obvious now, but I didn't think of it at the time. I wish I had done.

6

The next day it rained all morning and we couldn't go to Tom Tiddler's Ground. In the afternoon the sun came out, and we had just time to get there before it disappeared and the rain started again. We went into the cabin, and Brain and Sam and me started another game of Monopoly, with Darryl and Mary-Lou watching, and Mary-Lou poking her fingers into everything as usual. The game got a bit heated, and there was an argument about somebody having moved more than the right number of squares so as to avoid landing on somebody else's property. And in the middle of that we suddenly heard voices. Men's voices.

I looked out and saw two fellows standing on the bank, a big fellow and a little fellow. Next minute the big fellow started up the plank, and of course by now it wasn't booby-trapped, and in no time at all he'd flung the cabin door open and was staring in at us. With him being so big and the cabin so small and five of us in it already, there wasn't room for him inside. He grabbed hold of Darryl, who was nearest the door, and shoved him out, and nudged me to move up and let him sit on the bench, which meant Brain had to move off the other end. And then this fellow said, 'Bloody kids!', though we hadn't done anything to him at all.

The little fellow followed him in and said, 'What are you lot doing here?'

Mary-Lou piped up and said, 'It's our den.'

The big fellow said, '*Your* den? Hark at that, Roddy.'

48

The little fellow said to Sam, quite polite, 'Move up, love. Let your elders and betters sit down.' And there was him and the big one sitting at the table opposite each other, as if they'd taken over.

I realized that I knew who they were. They were the pair who worked the scrap-metal boat that we sometimes saw tied up at the Town Quay, just the other side of the Arches. They used to travel up and down the canal, dredging up old bikes and bedsteads and things that people had thrown in. My dad said this was a useful thing to do, and he didn't grudge them the money they made from it. But they also did a bit of dealing and door-to-door collecting, and Dad said they cheated people and gave them next to nothing for what they bought. He also reckoned they had something to do with disappearances of lead flashings from roofs and so on, though they'd never been caught. They had a big filthy boat that they carted scrap in, and a little glass-fibre one with an outboard motor that they used for buzzing around on business or going to canalside pubs.

My dad didn't think much of them, I knew. I didn't like the look of them either, at close quarters. The little fellow was thin-faced and sharp-eyed and crafty-looking. The big one had small eyes in a big red beefy face.

'What you looking at me like that for?' said the big fellow.

'I was thinking I know you,' I said. 'You have the scrap-metal boat.'

'That's right, lad,' said the little one. 'Huckle and Company. I'm Roddy Huckle. Rick's the Company.'

'And you can get out of here!' Rick added.

'Why should we?' said Sam, sharpish. 'It *is* our den! It was all derelict, and we fixed it up!'

Mary-Lou, who was clutching Nelson, snuggled up close to Sam and for once in her life didn't say anything. Brain was quietly picking up the Monopoly pieces. Rick swept his hand across the board in an absent-minded way and sent cards and dice and Monopoly money flying all over the place. Brain didn't react to that, and I didn't blame him, because he was well within Rick's reach, and I reckoned a big, bad-tempered fellow like him wouldn't think twice about clouting a kid.

But Sam didn't seem scared. She asked, 'Was it you who were here before?'

Rick said, 'What if it was?', but Roddy said quickly, 'No, it wasn't.'

Sam said, 'You made a mess, didn't you? And what happened to our things? What have you done with Vic's radio?'

Rick stared at Sam. His brain, supposing he had one, seemed to work very slowly. It took a while for the message to get through. But you could see that it registered in the end, and then he was furious. He made a movement as if he was just going to knock Sam into the middle of next week. And I expect he was, but luckily Roddy nipped in and said, 'Hold it, Rick!' And Roddy said to Sam, 'You've got it wrong, girlie! We haven't taken anybody's radio. Someone else must have been here.'

Rick got the idea and said, 'That's right. Somebody else musta been here. We haven't took your radio. Nor the chess-set neither.'

He didn't seem to see that he'd given the game away. Roddy saw all right, but maybe he hoped *we* hadn't. Anyway, he said, very smooth, 'If you left things here and they've gone, it's just too bad, but it's nothing to do with us.'

Mary-Lou could see that Sam wasn't afraid of these two, so she got quite bold and said, 'Nelson says it was you. He *saw* you.'

''Oo's Nelson?' asked Rick, looking round.

'*This* is Nelson,' said Mary-Lou, holding him up.

'A flipping teddy-bear!' said Rick. He went on, as if he'd just made a discovery, 'Flipping teddy-bears can't *see* owt or *say* owt.'

'Nelson can,' said Mary-Lou. And then, getting all cocky, she went on, 'This is our place. It's Tom Tiddler's Ground. You know what we're doing here? Picking up gold and silver!' And she chanted, 'Picking up gold and *sil*-ver!'

'Don't be daft, Mary-Lou!' said Sam. But Roddy had pricked up his ears.

'What was that, love?' he said to Mary-Lou, and grinned, the way a snake might grin if snakes could grin. 'You been finding something around here?'

'Nothing,' said Sam.

'Ooh, Sam, we *have*!' said Mary-Lou. Sam tried to shut her up, but it was no use. 'We found *money*!' she said. 'And a silver spoon. And a gold horsy thing.'

Rick just sat there. Probably he hadn't taken this in. But Roddy said, 'Money, love? That's interesting. How much?'

Brain said, 'She did find some money, but it was only pennies. And the spoon and the horse-brass are junk.'

'They're not! They're not!' cried Mary-Lou. 'They're *valuable*! The spoon's real silver and the horsy thing's gold!'

I didn't like the way this conversation was going. Nor, I could see, did Sam or Brain. It looked as if Mary-Lou could be getting us into difficulties. And she went on to make things worse by saying, 'And there might be more where they came from!'

'What about my radio?' I said, trying to change the subject.

Rick got to his feet, scowling, and I could see that in about half a millisecond he was going to give me the only answer I would ever get, which was a clout that would half kill me. But once again Roddy stopped him.

'Show me the silver spoon, love,' he said to Mary-Lou, all friendly.

Mary-Lou had it in her shorts pocket. She produced it.

Roddy looked at it for about ten seconds. 'Very nice,' he said, and gave it back to her. 'And the horse-brass? Is that it, on the shelf?'

He went to the shelf, picked it up and looked at it. I thought at first he wasn't much interested. Then he looked at it closer.

'An uncommon one, that,' he said. 'A sun-god's eye.' He took a clasp-knife out of his pocket and poked the horse-brass, back and front, with a sharp-pointed gadget. Then he said to Mary-Lou, 'Where did you say you found it?'

Mary-Lou hadn't said where she found it, but now she answered, all innocent, 'In the bottom of the boat.'

Roddy said, 'It's junk all right, but I like the design. I'm having it.'

'Hey! You can't do that!' I told him.

Roddy turned to me, and he didn't look nearly so friendly. His voice was smooth and cold.

'You listen to me!' he said. 'I've been patient with you, but

there's a limit. You kids know you've no right to be here. You're trespassing.'

'Yes,' said Sam, and then, cheeky-like, 'and so are you!'

Rick made a move again, and Roddy told him to sit down. Then Roddy said, 'I'd better explain to you, hadn't I? This boat belongs to me. And the land it's on, as well.'

That startled us all right.

'Don't look so surprised,' Roddy said. 'You must have known it belonged to somebody. All land belongs to somebody. Well, this was my grandad's. He owned the boat, too. He died years ago, poor old sod. I still miss him.'

Sam said boldly, 'I don't believe you.'

'Watch it, young lady!' said Roddy. 'You've said enough to be going on with.'

'Nelson doesn't believe you, either,' said Mary-Lou.

'And you've said enough, too,' said Roddy. 'I've told you, this land was my grandfather's. His name was Huckle, same as

mine. Gilbert Huckle. And anything that's found here belongs to me.'

Rick was gaping at Roddy, the same as we were. I was sure this was the first he'd heard of Gilbert Huckle or of owning the land. I wondered how stupid Roddy thought we were.

'And now,' Roddy went on, colder than ever, in fact quite nasty, 'be warned. You'll get out of here this minute, and you'll stay out. If I find you here again, you'll be in the Juvenile Court!'

'If there's anything left of you,' Rick added.

'So go on!' said Roddy. 'Get!'

From the look in Rick's eye, I guessed that if Brain or I had said anything more about the radio or the chess-set, he'd have clobbered us. So we didn't. But Mary-Lou wasn't keeping quiet.

'I want my horsy thing!' she wailed.

She got away without being clobbered, but she didn't get the horse-brass back. Roddy said, 'I've told you, it's not yours, it's mine.' Then he seemed to relent a little. 'I'll give you a reward for finding it,' he said. He felt in his pocket and gave her a fifty-pence piece.

'I don't want fifty pence, I want my horsy thing,' said Mary-Lou.

'Shut. Up,' said Roddy, quiet but real vicious. Mary-Lou looked at his face and then at Rick's, and I guess she knew when she was beaten, same as we all did. She didn't say anything more. Next minute we were all trooping down the gangplank. I went last, and I half expected to feel Rick's boot in my backside. I admit, I was scared stiff of that fellow, and so would you have been.

Anyway, nothing more happened. We walked away from the canal-boat to where our own little boat was moored.

Rick and Roddy had arrived at Tom Tiddler's Ground in their glass-fibre runabout with the outboard motor. We knew that, because it was tied up close to our own boat. And Darryl was there, waiting for us. We'd forgotten all about him. He looked nervous, and hurried us up to get aboard and on our way, but once we were out in the middle of the canal he started giggling.

'What have you got to laugh about?' asked Brain, who was rowing.

Darryl went on giggling. In the end I took him by the shoulders. '*Tell us!*' I said.

'I put water in their fuel tank!' said Darryl.

I started laughing, but stopped when I saw that Brain and Sam didn't think it was funny. Not one bit, they didn't.

'They'll murder us if they ever catch us *now*!' said Brain.

7

Brain rowed fast, all the way back to the Arches, in case Rick
and Roddy came after us, though actually we reckoned that by
the time they'd got back to their boat and struggled to start it
and taken to the oars they wouldn't have much chance of
catching us up. And in fact we didn't see any more of them
that day.

We talked about them, of course, all the way back. We
didn't believe a word of what Roddy had said about his
grandad owning the land. But Brain and Sam didn't think we
should go there any more. I said that the canal was twenty-odd
miles long, and that Rick and Roddy worked their way up and
down it, and most of the time they weren't at our end. But
Brain said there was always a risk that they'd turn up, and
Sam said, all fierce, 'If you think I'm going to take any chances
with Mary-Lou you've got another think coming!' And Sam
and Brain both said the den had been spoiled for us now, and it
wouldn't be the same if we *did* go there, and anyway there was
only about a week of the school holidays left.

Mary-Lou kicked up no end of a fuss. She wanted to go back
when those two naughty men had gone, she said, and find
some more gold and silver. I said Brain and Sam were scared,
which made them really mad. And we had a right old argy-
bargy, but Darryl sided with the other two and in the end they
got their way, and it looked as if that was the end of Tom
Tiddler's Ground for us. We made friends again before we
reached the Arches, but we were all so miserable about what

had happened that when Sam and Mary-Lou went home for their dinner, and Darryl went off to wherever Darryl goes when he isn't with us, we didn't make any arrangements to meet afterwards.

I'd have gone for my dinner too, but Brain said, 'Hang on a minute. We want a word with your dad.'

I said, 'What's the point? We've lost out, haven't we? The less we say to my dad the better.'

Brain said, 'We haven't lost out yet.'

I said, 'That's not what you were saying a few minutes ago.'

Brain said, 'Well, we can't go to Tom Tiddler's Ground again, at least not with Mary-Lou. But we're not letting those two fellows get away with it. And Roddy was a bit too interested in that horse-brass he took off us. Maybe it's a genuine old one, worth pounds.'

It crossed my mind again that there was something odd about that brass, but I still couldn't put my finger on it.

'I reckon,' said Brain, 'that the only person who can do anything about those two fellows is the person who *does* own Tom Tiddler's Ground, and we should try to find out who he is. And we begin by asking your dad.'

'My dad won't want to get involved,' I said.

'That's all right,' said Brain. 'We won't *ask* him to get involved. We'll just ask him about the land.'

So we went to my dad's place and asked him. And the first thing my dad said was, 'Why do you want to know?'

Brain said, 'It's research. We got really interested in that old boat. We'd like to find out more about it, if the present owner would tell us.'

Well, that was a pretty good line to take with my dad, who's always going on about old times. For the next half-hour we had him telling us about the days when there might be anything up to a dozen canal-boats tied up at the Town Quay and a dozen more at the East Basin, where now there's none. And he

told us all sorts of stories about the canal people, going back years and years, and some of them being stories that his dad and grandad had told *him*.

Brain listened, very interested-seeming, while I tried not to yawn, because I'd heard all the stories before, some of them two or three times. After a while, Brain got my dad back to the subject of the old boat and Tom Tiddler's Ground and who owned it. And my dad looked a bit uneasy and said he didn't know.

That was a surprise. My dad hates to admit that there's *anything* about old times in Claypits that he doesn't know. And usually he *does* know.

Brain looked crestfallen. And then my dad said, 'Well, there's somebody around who *does* know something about that, though whether she'll tell you what she knows is another question.' And Brain said, 'Who?' And Dad said, 'Vic's gran. You'd better go and talk to her.'

I groaned aloud at that. I see enough of Gran without going and asking for it. I wasn't sure I wouldn't rather drop the whole thing. I said to Brain, '*You* can go and talk to Gran.' Dad frowned at that and said, 'You can both go. Gran often complains that she only has one grandson and she doesn't see much of him.' And then he added rather quickly, before I could sneak off, 'Don't go away, either of you. She has a telephone. I'll ring her now, this minute.'

And Brain *thanked* him. There's times when I could *crucify* Brain.

Gran was at home. Gran's always at home if she isn't at our house. I could hear Dad talking to her, but I couldn't hear what he was saying. I was fairly hopeful that Gran wouldn't want to see us, because from the way Gran talks about boys you'd think she would rather have a family of Great Apes around the place than a boy. But no luck. Dad was soon back to say that Gran wanted both of us to come to tea that same afternoon. Four-thirty sharp, as Gran had her tea early. 'And don't be late,' said Dad. 'You know what your gran's like.'

Oh yes, I know what Gran's like.

Well, on this particular day, she wasn't like it. At least, she wasn't like it with Brain. She was as nice as pie with Brain. Mind you, she still didn't talk to me, she talked to Brain *about* me, even if she was asking a question that I had to answer.

Anyway, she'd laid on an enormous tea. She must have been all afternoon working on it. There was ham and tongue and sausage rolls, and then there was bread and jam and sponge-cake. And Brain was as polite as anything, and Gran said, 'Somebody's taught you table manners, Brian. I wish *all* lads were taught how to behave like you've been.' And she threw a dirty look at me across the table. I was cross and said, 'I've been saying please and thank you, too,' and Gran said to Brain, 'I wish he wouldn't mumble,' meaning me.

Then I got really furious, when Gran said to Brain, 'He's

leaving crusts on his plate. When I was a lass we ate up our crusts and thought ourselves lucky to have them.' So I said, real furious, 'I wasn't leaving that crust, I was going to eat it in a minute,' and Gran said to Brain, '*You* wouldn't speak to your gran the way *he* does, would you?'

But I've got to hand it to Brain, he was managing the old girl a treat. He had her smiling at him and even patting his hand. You could tell she thought he was the greatest, and it was going to keep her happy for weeks, every time she came to our house, telling my mum how much better-behaved Brain was than me.

Of course, Gran knew more about Brain's family than he did himself. She remembered his Great-Uncle Ernest, who was bedridden for thirty years and had a lovely funeral, and his Great-Aunt Mabel, who was crippled with rheumatism, and his Great-Uncle George, who was knocked down by a tramcar and lost his wits, and his Great-Uncle Arthur, who retired with a gold watch after fifty years at work and died the following week, and it seems like Brain had hundreds of relatives, all known to Gran, and all having dreadful things happening to them non-stop. Then Gran finished, 'Those were the good old days,' and Brain got his chance and asked her about Tom Tiddler's Ground and the canal-boat.

And this stopped Gran short. I guess my dad hadn't told her exactly what we were after. That would be just like him. He won't get involved in things if he can help it, and he won't talk about delicate subjects. And you could see from the startled way Gran reacted that this was a very delicate subject. Her mouth opened and closed once or twice without anything coming out. Then she said, slow and quiet, in a voice I'd never heard from her before, 'That's going back a bit, Brian.'

Brain waited. I'd been wishing we could get away, but suddenly I could feel there was something important in the air.

Gran said, 'Yes, I know who bought Tom Tiddler's Ground when the canal company sold it. It was a man who owned his

own boat and had a cottage there, where the Throughway is now. He'd worked hard and done well, had Reuben Oakley. And . . . he had a son.'

Gran was quiet for a minute, then said, 'It was before I met your grandpa, Vic.' I think that was the first time Gran had spoken to me directly for weeks, maybe months. She sounded quite different from usual. 'It was a long time ago. A long, long time ago. Your grandpa and me were married forty years, and it's four years now since he died.'

Brain and me went on waiting, not saying anything. Then Gran said, real fierce, 'Ben was a *good* lad. He didn't do it. I know he didn't do it.'

There were tears in Gran's eyes. Brain said, gentle-like, '*Who* didn't do *what*?'

Gran said, 'Reuben Oakley was killed. They pulled his body out of the canal. But he wasn't drowned, he died of head injuries. His son – who was another Reuben, but he was always

61

called Ben – was charged with murdering him. Everybody knew they'd had a great row. It was over a lass. Ben wanted to wed her, and his dad didn't want him to. Ben stormed out one day, and every boatman in the basin knew he'd gone. A day or two later, Reuben disappeared too. Folk thought maybe he'd gone looking for Ben. And then ... like I say, they found Reuben's body in the cut. And Ben was tried for murder.'

'And you said he didn't do it?' said Brain.

'He was found not guilty. There wasn't the evidence to convict him. Reuben had been drinking hard in the Rose and Castle for a couple of nights after Ben left, and they said he could have fell off the quay and hit his head on the way down. The injuries didn't prove it either way.'

'Well, if Ben was found not guilty, wasn't that the end of the matter?' asked Brain.

'No, it wasn't. For one thing, Reuben was supposed to have saved a bit, but his money was never found. There was some that reckoned Ben had killed him and made off with it, and that he never said what had happened to it because that would have given him away. There was others that said maybe Ben hadn't actually killed his dad, but that all the same it was his fault that Reuben died. And Ben himself was one of those. I doubt if he ever forgave himself.'

'And what happened to the girl?' said Brain.

'He didn't marry her. After all that, they thought they couldn't. It wouldn't have seemed right. She ... married somebody else.'

'What about Ben?' I asked.

'Ben sold the cottage, but he kept his dad's boat, and he worked it for years. Not on this canal, though. He couldn't bear to be in Claypits, after what had happened. He only came here once more that I know of, and that was when the boat was wore out. He brought it back to his dad's land as its last resting-place, you might say. They tell me it's still there, what's left of it.'

'And is Ben still alive?' I asked.

'So far as I know, he is. But don't ask me where. I haven't seen Ben since the day I wed your grandpa, and I don't expect to see him again this side of the grave.'

Brain asked, 'Would anybody know where Ben is now?'

Gran said, 'Nobody except maybe Luke.' And Brain said, 'Who's Luke?' And Gran said, 'Luke Fillery.' And me and Brain looked at each other but we were neither of us any the wiser, because we hadn't heard of Luke Fillery.

'Luke worked as Reuben Oakley's lad, and then with Ben, until he got a boat of his own. And *he* might be dead now. If he's alive he'll be *really* old, ten years older than I am, and I'm not as young as I'd like to be.'

'Where would we find him?' Brain asked.

Gran didn't know. When she'd last heard of him, Luke had been living with his son and his son's wife in a little street in the Jungle. But they couldn't be there now, because there wasn't any Jungle left. The Jungle was a slummy part of the city, not far from the Claypits district, and it was nicknamed the Jungle because the streets in it had fancy names like Orchid Grove and Mimosa Row. It's all been pulled down now.

'The folk that lived there were moved out to Scarsholme Estate,' said Gran. Then suddenly her voice got all suspicious, and she said, 'What do you want to know all this for, anyroad?'

Brain said, innocent-like, 'We saw that boat and wondered who it belonged to, that's all.'

Gran said to Brain, 'So you asked his dad' (she was back to calling me 'him' again) 'and his dad sent you to ask *me*. Oh well, I suppose there's no reason why he shouldn't. What's done is done, and it was all a long time ago. And now, Brian, you've not been eating. Have a bit more of that cake. *He's* had plenty.'

She meant me, of course. She'd been watching me all the time. Gran never misses anything. But I hadn't had all *that* much cake. Only three pieces.

8

'Well?' I said. 'Satisfied?'

'Sure,' said Brain. 'Your gran's all right, isn't she? Wish I had one like her.'

'You can have her,' I said.

'Oh, come *on*. She means well. A bit sharpish, that's all. You'll be worse when you're her age. Anyway, it was a good tea.'

'And what do we do now?' I asked.

'We'll find this Luke Fillery, if he's alive. Shouldn't be hard, with a name like that. I never heard of anybody called Fillery before.'

'I bet Scarsholme's full of them,' I said gloomily.

But when we looked in the telephone book, in our house next morning, we saw that there was only one Fillery in the whole city, and it was a Scarsholme address, which looked promising. My mum was upstairs vacuuming, and not likely to interrupt us. So when Brain suggested we ring the number right away, I told him to go ahead. Somehow, I wasn't too keen to do it myself. Brain is better than I am at dealing with grown-ups.

Standing beside him, I could just faintly hear a woman's voice answering at the other end. Brain asked for Luke Fillery. Said he wanted to ask Mr Fillery about canal life for a school project. (He crossed his fingers while he said this.)

I could hear that the voice was asking questions. Brain, very patient, explained who he was and what school he was at, and how the project had to be finished by the end of the holidays, next week. (His fingers were still crossed.) The voice went on a bit. Then Brain asked, 'Where *is* Peaceholme?' And, after a bit, very polite, 'Thank you. We'll go and see him there. Goodbye.'

Then Brain hung up, pulled a face, and said, 'That was his son's wife. She sounds a real old so-and-so. They've put him in an old folks' home.'

'And you're going to see him there?' I asked.

'*We* are.'

'Who says *I'm* coming?'

'Course you are. You're my pal, aren't you?'

'They mightn't let us in.'

'They will,' said Brain. 'The woman's telephoning them. Says the old guy'll be glad of a bit of company. She says she goes to see him when she can but she hasn't been able to make it lately. It's at Overley, the other side of the city. I bet it's *years* since she went.'

'I don't fancy it,' I said. I had a picture in my mind of some great big chilly institution with hundreds of poor old wrinklies sitting around waiting to die. But Brain said Peaceholme wasn't like that, it was one of about a dozen privately owned homes scattered around the city, where old folk went and the Council paid for them. 'The woman says it's very nice,' he said, 'and they can do their rooms up the way they want. Seems the old guy spent his savings on that, and she wasn't too pleased about it.'

'It's five or six miles to Overley,' I said, 'and it's hot again.'

'We've got bikes, haven't we?' said Brain. The fact is, once Brain gets going on something there's no stopping him.

So I sighed and got my bike out, and we went to Brain's for *his* bike, and who should we meet on the way but Sam? And Sam was beaming all over her face, because there was an empty space beside her where Mary-Lou usually was.

Mary-Lou had gone to stay at her aunt's for a couple of days. And Sam instantly offered to come with us. I didn't mind too much. I was getting used to Sam by now. Sam isn't too bad really. A bit bossy, that's all.

So Sam went to get *her* bike, and we trolleyed off up Camellia Hill and out along the main road to Overley, where we turned left at the Green and right at the Crown Inn, and we came to Peaceholme, which was just a big old house set back from the road. And the woman in charge of it was all right. She was called Mrs Hamley, and she'd been expecting us, and she smiled, all friendly, and said Mr Fillery would be glad to see us, and he was just the right person to tell us about canals, and we'd see why in a minute.

Peaceholme was a rambling old place, and it must have had about twenty rooms. Mrs Hamley led us up steps and along passages, and at last she knocked on a door and a voice from inside said, 'Come in.' And she said, 'You'll get a surprise when you do,' and went away and left us to it. Brain opened the door and we went in. And yes, we did get a surprise.

It wasn't like any room I'd ever seen before. It was small and crowded with stuff, all neatly organized. There was a bunk-bed with a locker under it, and a cupboard alongside full of gleaming crockery, with a door that had been let down to make a table. There was a polished black stove that wasn't lit but had a brass kettle and shiny pans hanging up behind. There were lace curtains on a pretend window with a picture of a castle and a bridge, and there were frilly-edged plates on the wall, and there was a wooden stool painted with roses and castles. And there were narrow shelves crammed with photographs and ornaments. And . . . a row of shining discs. Horse-brasses!

Up from the bunk got a little, thin, white-haired old man in a neat blue suit who looked at least eighty years old, if not ninety.

'Welcome aboard!' he said.

We were all staring around us.

'There, that surprised you, didn't it?' he said. 'I had the room done up special, like a canal-boat cabin, to make me feel at home. Now you know how it would have looked in the old days, when canal folk lived on their boats.'

I believed him. Just for a minute I really felt as if we might be afloat.

Brain told him who we were, and he shook hands with all of us. For such a frail-looking old guy, he had a pretty good grip. 'It's good to see some young faces,' he said. 'Or any faces at all, to tell you the truth. Mind you, they look after me well here, very well. And my daughter-in-law comes in when she can. But I wouldn't say I get too much company.'

He looked a bit sad as he said that, but then he smiled and said, 'Don't get me wrong. I'm not sorry for myself. And it's a good day today, seeing as I'm being useful. When you get to my age, you like to feel you can still be a bit of good to some-body. These school projects are important, aren't they? It's a great thing, education.'

I felt a bit ashamed that our project was only a pretend one, but it looked as if we were making Mr Fillery's day. He went on to tell us he couldn't always remember *recent* things but his memory was fine when it came to old times, 'clear as a bell'.

He told us about cargoes and locks and the old days of horse-drawn boats, which he remembered from the time when he started work on the canals as a lad not much older than we were now. It was a bit like my dad, except that I hadn't heard these stories before, whereas I've heard my dad's millions of times. After a while Brain let drop, very casual, that we'd seen the old boat in the inlet. That got Mr Fillery quite excited.

'You mean *Tiddler*!' he said.

We hadn't known what the boat was called. We'd realized

there must have been a name painted on it some time, but the paint had all worn off years ago.

Some tiddler, though!

'Was it called after Tom Tiddler?' asked Brain. 'Who *was* Tom Tiddler, anyway?'

Mr Fillery didn't know anything about Tom Tiddler, if there ever was such a person. He reckoned the boat was called *Tiddler* because it was berthed on Tom Tiddler's Ground, and maybe as a bit of a joke, seeing it was seventy-two feet long. And he remembered it very well, from having worked on it.

'The cabin of *Tiddler* was just like this,' he told us. 'She was a fine boat in her day.' And this gave me a very strange feeling. In my mind I kind of moved the old guy's room that we were sitting in to the old barge, and it was as if it was bringing it back to life.

Brain said, 'What happened to the man who owned it?'

That made the old man frown.

'Reuben Oakley died,' he said. 'It was a bad business. Then his son took *Tiddler* over. Young Ben. So far as I know, he's still alive, but I haven't seen him for years. He always avoided coming back to the canal basin here.'

'Because of the suspicion?' said Brain.

Luke Fillery shot Brain a sharp look.

'I see you've heard about that,' he said. 'Takes a long time for these things to be forgotten. Yes, even when he'd been found not guilty, young Ben reckoned that everyone was looking at him and wondering if he'd done it after all. He couldn't bear that. Mind you, them that really *knew* him knew he couldn't have done it in a month of Sundays. He was a fine strong young fellow, but he never raised a fist in anger. Sensitive, that was Ben. Too sensitive for his own good.'

Mr Fillery let out a great big sigh.

'There was those who asked what happened to old Reuben's savings. Well, I don't know that, but I can tell you one thing. Young Ben never had his dad's money. He never wanted it. Used to say it'd be tainted, after the court case.'

'Nobody ever found it, did they?' Brain asked.

'No. Never found to this day, that I know of. It's possible there wasn't any, but I think there was. Reuben had been a saving man all his life. It wouldn't have been a fortune, mind you, but it'd have been a useful bit. He must have tucked it away somewhere.'

'Wouldn't he have put it in the bank?' Brain asked.

'No. Old boatmen like Reuben didn't go in much for banking. They liked to keep their own hands on their money, if they had any.'

'So he might have hidden it on the boat?' I asked.

'Maybe, maybe not. The police searched the boat when he died, and never found nothing. Mind you, there's so many hiding-places on a seventy-two-foot working boat, you couldn't check them all without you took the whole boat to bits. They didn't do that, and nor would young Ben have done afterwards.'

'Mr Fillery,' said Sam, who hadn't said anything so far, 'the weather has taken it to bits by now.'

That made us all think. Mr Fillery was quiet for a minute. He was looking a bit suspicious. 'What are you getting at?' he asked. 'What are you youngsters up to?'

'Let's come clean,' said Brain. 'We found a jar with old pennies in the bottom of the boat. Also a horse-brass.'

'Show me!' said Luke Fillery. Well, we couldn't. But Brain told him about the pennies and how we'd spent them in the museum, and about the horse-brass and how Roddy had taken it off us.

'I remember the jar of pennies,' he said. 'Reuben kept them for spending along the way. You could get a lot for a penny in those days. As for the horse-brass, that's interesting. Very interesting. Reuben had a few of them. He didn't *collect* them, like folk do now. They came off horses he'd owned. Pity you had to let it go. What was it like?'

We did our best to describe the pattern. And you could see that the old guy was getting even more excited. 'A sun in splendour!' he said. 'I recall the very one. It was a face-piece, that was, hung on the horse's forehead. Some of the boatmen thought that if the horse wore a flash there it kept off the Evil Eye.'

'My little sister said it was gold,' said Sam.

'No. There was a special sort of brass called pinchbeck that was sometimes used for horse-brasses. You could burnish it to look like gold.'

'So it wouldn't be valuable?' I asked.

'Might be worth a few pounds, a genuine old horse-brass. I don't really know, I'm out of touch. Still . . . you said you found it in the bottom of the boat?'

'Yes,' said Brain. 'Covered with mud and stuff.'

'And you don't know what else might be there. But let me tell you, anything that's found belongs to young Ben. Nobody else has any claim on it, and that includes you!'

We nodded.

'That understood? Right! Well, now, listen to me. Like I said just now, there's any number of hiding-places on a canal-boat. For instance, not going any further than the cabin itself, you could hide something under the steps that lead down from the back deck, or you could put a false bottom in a locker or a false back to a cupboard or . . . I could go on for a long time. But this young lady' – he looked at Sam – 'is right. If something was hid and nobody found it, it'd finish up in the bilges in the end, when the boat rotted away. So you never know, there *could* be money to be found. Sovereigns, most like . . . It's a pity those two fellows have poked their noses in. Do you think they're after it?'

'They could be,' I said.

'Then I reckon you should go and find young Ben,' said Mr Fillery.

'That's what we want to do,' said Brain. 'That's why we came to see you.'

'There never was no school project, eh?' said Mr Fillery. 'You crafty young devils!' He didn't seem to mind. 'Well now, I think of Ben Oakley as young Ben, but he's not all that young really. Not now. The last I heard was that he'd retired and gone to live on a boat he owns at Southerly Junction.'

'Where's Southerly Junction?' Brain asked.

'It's a canal junction. Where this canal joins the Potteries and Black Country. Twenty or thirty miles away. If Ben's alive and still there, and if you can find him, I reckon you should get him over here as soon as possible. If he'll come. And listen, if you do find Ben, remind him of his old pal and workmate. There's a few things *I* still want to do in this life. One of them's to see Ben again, and another is to make one more trip round the canal system. And there isn't much time for that before I die.'

'You're not going to die just yet,' said Sam.

'No good talking like that, my dear. The young think they'll live for ever, but at my age you know better . . . Here, just a minute.' Luke rummaged in a drawer. 'Here's a canal map. It'll help you find Southerly Junction. Good luck to you, you young frauds. School project, eh? School project! The things kids get up to, these days!'

9

Sounds like a big important place, doesn't it, Southerly Junction? Well, I expect it was, long ago, when the canals were all full of horse-drawn boats. But now you wouldn't find it at all on an ordinary map. It's where the North-west Junction Canal joins the Potteries and Black Country. Both of these canals run through the back parts of a whole string of industrial towns, and if you were looking for a nice place for a picnic you'd look as far away from any of them as you could get.

So when me and Brain said we wanted to go there next morning for a day out on the bikes, our mums thought we were out of our minds. Maybe we should have told them we were heading for the moors, which were in the opposite direction. But Brain persuaded them that canals were history and education and all that, so we didn't have to work on them too hard, and they gave us packed lunches and told us a hundred and seventy-seven times to be careful, and I expect they were glad to be rid of us for the day. Sam didn't have to persuade her mum or anything, her mum being at work, so she just made up her own lunch and left a note on the kitchen table in case her mum was back before she was, and off we all went.

By mid-morning it was getting hot again, and there's nowhere that gets so hot as streets in towns, and we had to ride twenty-odd miles of town roads, mostly paved with stone setts, which are little lumps of stone specially arranged so as to shake cyclists to pieces. The special map Mr Fillery had given us showed the canal as a thick blue line running all the way from

73

Claypits to Southerly Junction, but actually we hardly ever saw it. Sometimes we were quite close, but it was always at the other side of factories or warehouses or something. Once we crossed it on a bridge, and I can tell you it wasn't blue, it was black, and looked as thick as treacle. Further on we crossed it again, and there was a pleasure-boat chugging along, with folk sunbathing on the roof. Just like the South of France, except for the scenery.

I have to admit, I got a bit fed up with the ride. So would you have done, by the time you'd been slogging your guts out in the heat for a couple of hours. But Brain went doggedly on, cycling first in line, Sam with her head down following him, and me bringing up the rear, cursing and swearing a bit, getting hotter and crosser and wondering if we'd have any luck when we got to Southerly Junction, if we ever did.

And when we got there, we didn't realize at first that we *had* got there. We were on a busy road, about a mile from a town centre, and lots of buildings all around had been pulled down, and there was a mixture of big shiny new ones with what was left of the small scruffy tumbledown ones. We asked half a dozen people the way to Southerly Junction, and they just stared at us. Never heard of it, they said. So we pored over the map together, and Brain said, 'It ought to be right here. Look, there's a church behind us and a traffic roundabout ahead, and the canal should be alongside that road.' But there was nothing alongside the road except a high blank wall.

Then Sam said, 'There's an opening in the wall.' And so there was. It didn't look anything much, like it might be the way into somebody's backyard. It was only wide enough for one person. But we leaned our bikes on the wall and peered through the opening, one after another. And it was the way into another world.

You wouldn't believe it if you hadn't seen it. There was a flight of stone steps leading down from the opening, and at the bottom a wide basin of water opened out, and there was quays and gravel paths and little funny footbridges and a lock and a lock-keeper's cottage and a garden full of flowers and a white-walled old pub called the Navigation. And you could see that it really was a junction, because one canal ran right through the basin and out the other side, and the other canal ran into it under the road and through the lock.

And all round the basin, boats were moored. Some of them were plastic cruisers, but most were big long narrow-boats like the one at Tom Tiddler's Ground, only they were freshly painted and brightly coloured and shipshape, and they had cabins running the full length of the boat, not just little ones at the back like ours.

We locked the three bikes together and left them by the opening, and then we went down and started walking round the canal basin. Nobody asked us who we were or what we were doing there. Some of the boats were locked up, but there were people on board others, and some were being painted or swabbed down. The people didn't look like boatmen, though. They looked like holidaymakers. They seemed to be having a good time, and they waved or shouted hello to us. Some of them were sitting out on the back decks having their lunch, and we realized that we were hungry.

'Let's eat first and look for Ben Oakley after that,' said Brain. So we found a bench, and we opened our packets and swapped our food around and munched, and swigged orange drink from a bottle that Sam had brought, and watched the boats moving in and out of the basin and through the lock. It began to seem like quite a good outing. Although I'd been thinking all the way to Southerly Junction that we probably wouldn't find Ben Oakley anyway, by the time we'd finished eating I thought we probably would. It's funny how food cheers you up.

Brain scrunched our wrapping-papers together and put them

in a bin along with the empty bottle, and we set to work. The obvious thing was to ask people about Ben Oakley, but none of those we spoke to had heard of him. They were only holiday-makers passing through, they said. They didn't know anything about people *living* here. No luck so far.

It was Sam's idea that we should ask at the lock cottage, and it was Brain who did it. And that put us on the right track. The lock-keeper was a little thin man with a big grin, and he was helpful. Yes, he knew Ben Oakley, he said. He'd known old Ben for years. We should look for a boat called *Ellen* at the permanent moorings, in the far corner of the basin.

So off we went and found the permanent moorings, where there were about a dozen boats tied up side by side with their front ends to the quay and their rears sticking out into the basin. Nearly all of them seemed to be closed down and locked up. The last one in line, the freshest and brightest of the canal-boats we'd seen, had the name painted on it in fancy capital

letters: ELLEN.

But there was no sign of life aboard *Ellen*. We clambered from the quay to the front deck and knocked on the cabin door. No answer. We tried the door, and it was locked. There was a catwalk along the outside of the boat, and as nobody seemed to be watching us we edged our way along it to the back deck, where there was another door into the cabin. That one was locked, too. We worked our way back to the front, and were just going to jump down on to the quay when an elderly geezer came bustling up, carrying a plastic shopping-bag in each hand, and he put them down on the quay and stood there waiting for us, looking very fierce.

'Can I help you?' this geezer asked, in a tone of voice as if the help he had in mind was a clip over the earhole. Then, in case we hadn't got the message, he spelled it out differently: 'What are you kids doing here?'

We were awkwardly placed, because we couldn't jump off

the boat without landing straight in front of him. He looked at us and we looked back, nervous-like.

'Were you trying to break in?' he asked us, still fierce.

'N-no, sir,' said Brain. And suddenly the old guy burst out laughing.

'I'm not going to eat you,' he said. 'Kids always want to nose around a boat like this. Do you want a ride?'

And now I could see that in spite of looking so fierce he wasn't a bad old guy. He was pretty old, but not as old as Luke, and though he was tall and thin and stooped a bit, he was kind of tough and stringy too. He had a brown face with heavy lines in it, and bright blue eyes with wrinkles at the corners, and a lot of white hair. And he had to be Ben Oakley.

I wondered if Brain was going to tell him right away what we'd come for, but all Brain said to the offer of a ride was, 'Yes, please.' Ben Oakley handed the bag of shopping up to me, and untied the front of the boat, and then swung himself on to the front deck as light and easy as if he was a monkey in a tree, and said, 'You'd better come through the cabin.'

We followed him inside, and his cabin was about five times as big as the one on *Tiddler*, because it ran all the length of the boat. Ben Oakley had a front sitting-room with a gas fire, and a kitchen with a cooker and fridge, and a shower-room, and a back cabin with a real bed in it, and you'd hardly have known you were on a boat at all if it wasn't for all the roses and castles and fancy decorations that canal folk go in for.

He took us out on the back deck and started up his diesel engine and backed the boat out into the basin and did some smart work with the tiller, and in no time at all we were chugging along a bit of the main canal. I was just thinking that the steering looked a bit tricky, like steering a row of cottages, and steering them from behind at that, when Ben Oakley said, 'Want to have a go?' and passed me the tiller. And we all had a go in turn.

I didn't do too badly. It wasn't my fault that another boat came round a bend too fast and bumped us, but Ben Oakley said it didn't matter, these boats were built to take a bump or two. I was cross that Brain and Sam didn't bump anything, though, when it was their turn.

We only went about a mile, and then there was a place where the canal widened, and Ben took the tiller and did some more fancy work, going into forward and reverse half a dozen times each, so as to turn this great long boat around. And back we went to the basin. We'd only been out about half an hour, but it was good. When we'd tied up, Ben lifted part of the back deck and showed us the engine, which Sam got all excited about, though to me it was just a diesel engine.

You could tell Ben Oakley enjoyed showing us things. I bet he'd shown hundreds of kids round the boat in his time. He was a cheerful kind of fellow who told jokes and laughed a good deal and whistled. I liked him. When Sam asked if he was happy living alone, Ben said he'd been doing it for years and it suited him fine. 'So long as I have my health and my wits, I'm all right,' he said, 'and they're not failing yet.' And he certainly looked pretty fit to me.

He didn't seem in a hurry to get rid of us. But I was thinking it was time we got down to business. And I have to admit, Brain led up to it very neatly. All he said was, 'Thank you very much, Mr Oakley.' And Ben looked surprised and asked, 'How did you know my name?' And Brain said, 'We've been talking to Luke Fillery.'

'So you know Luke Fillery? Why didn't you tell me?' Ben Oakley asked, and then, sounding a bit anxious, 'Is Luke all right? He's not ill or anything?'

I said, 'He isn't ill. Just old.'

Ben Oakley said, 'I expect he thinks it's time I went to see him. Well, so it is. Anyway, what's all this about? What brought you here?'

Brain said, 'It's about your dad's money.'

We'd certainly startled people with our inquiries. First Gran, then Luke Fillery, and now it was Ben Oakley's turn. He looked quite shaken. He didn't say anything at first, then he said in a very quiet voice, 'You'd better come into the cabin.' We followed him through the boat and sat ourselves down where he pointed, on the seats.

I'll always remember the next few minutes. Not just for what was said, but as a kind of scene that comes into my mind from time to time, very sharp and clear. The doors at each end of the boat were open for the heat, and from where I sat I could see out both ways. In one direction there was the canal basin and the buildings at the far side of it, and in the other direction was the quay and the lock, and there were sounds of somebody's radio and of kids playing and of someone coming through the lock and yelling instructions. All quite ordinary. But here in the cabin it felt tense. As if the air was loaded. Brain and Sam and me sat watching Ben Oakley's face and waiting for him to say something. He had a strange expression, as if suddenly there was a sad man looking out from behind the cheerful one.

At last Ben said, still very quiet, 'I suppose you come from Claypits?'

We all nodded.

Ben said, bitter-sounding, 'I did all I could to get away from that place, but there's some things you can't leave behind. Now listen, it's nearly fifty years since my dad died. Who's talking about his money?'

'Mr Fillery thought he might have hidden it on his boat,' said Brain.

'On *Tiddler*? That's an old story. There were some who believed it, but I wasn't one of them. I don't know why Luke should revive it now. Putting ideas into your heads.'

'We *found* some things that Mr Fillery said were your dad's,' Brain told him.

'Oh,' said Ben Oakley. He still sounded a bit shaken. Not at all pleased. 'What did you find?' he asked. 'And where?'

'A jar of old pennies and a horse-brass. In the bottom of the boat. In the mud.'

There was a long silence. Then, 'They could be my dad's. He always kept a jar of pennies, and he had a few horse-brasses at one time. But what if they *were* his? What does it matter, after all these years?'

'Mr Fillery thought there might be other things that had finished up in the bilges when the boat rotted. Including the savings that were never found. And it wasn't only *him* that was interested.'

'Who else?' Ben Oakley asked, sharpish.

'Roddy Huckle and his pal. The scrap dealers.'

'I don't know Roddy, but I know the Huckle family. A bad lot. The less you have to do with Huckles the better, we used to say. Well, come on, you'd better tell me all about it. What were you doing, fishing around in *Tiddler*?'

So we told him how we'd come upon the old boat and how we'd repaired the cabin to make a den, and about Mary-Lou's finds and what Rick and Roddy had done. Ben Oakley sat there, very still and quiet, seeming a different person from the one who'd given us joyrides and laughed and whistled. Once or twice I saw him looking at my face in a funny kind of way, as if there was something about it that puzzled him. And when we told him what Gran had said, he turned to me and asked, 'What's your gran's name?'

'Mrs Horrocks,' I said.

'I mean her *first* name.'

I never think of Gran as having a first name. I call her Gran and my parents call her Mum. But she does have a name, of course, the same as anyone else. 'It's Ellen,' I said.

'I thought so,' said Ben Oakley. 'I remember her well. How *is* she these days?'

'Oh, she's all right. Complains a bit about her rheumatism.'

'We none of us get any younger,' said Ben. Then, 'It's true what your gran says. I was charged with killing my father.'

'But she said you didn't do it. You were found not guilty.'

'That's right,' said Ben. 'I didn't do it. But he died, and it was my fault in a way. If I hadn't had that row with him and walked out, it wouldn't have happened. It wasn't like him at all to drink too much and fall off a quay, the way he did. I'll tell you something. In all the years since they found him dead, there hasn't been a day that I haven't thought about it. Now, let's have a good look at you, young Vic. There's something of your gran in your face, isn't there?'

I wasn't too pleased at that. 'They say I'm more like my gramp,' I told him.

'And how's *he* getting on?'

'He's dead. Died four years ago.'

That seemed to startle Ben Oakley some more.

'I didn't know that!' he said. 'Let's see, they had two children, didn't they?'

'Yes,' I said. 'My dad and Uncle Sid.'

Ben Oakley gave me a sad kind of look and said he'd never married, nor had any children or grandchildren that he knew of. I nearly told him that Gran wasn't all that thrilled with having *me*, but I thought I'd better not.

'If she'd married ... someone else,' he said, 'you'd have been a different person entirely.' Then he gave me an even odder look, and said, 'I oughtn't to wish that, ought I?'

I didn't know what he was talking about. For a minute or so, the four of us just sat there, not saying anything. It was really strange. There were all sorts of sounds floating in from the canal basin outside, and yet inside the cabin it felt *silent*. Then at last Ben Oakley said to all of us, 'What do you want me to do?'

'Well,' said Brain, 'it's your land, and your boat, and I

suppose the things Mary-Lou found were yours. And if there *is* money there, that must be yours, too. We don't want Rick and Roddy to get it. Maybe if you came back to Claypits for a while we could help you find it.'

Ben Oakley said, 'There may not *be* any. I never did think my dad had money, in spite of what folk said. I was more surprised at the time that his horse-brasses weren't found than that there wasn't any money. He really valued those horse-brasses.'

Sam said, 'Mary-Lou thought the one she found was gold, but Mr Fillery said it couldn't be.'

Ben smiled. 'They looked like gold,' he said. 'But I'm afraid Luke was right. Boatmen and carters liked their horse-brasses to look like gold, and sometimes they were made of a special brass with more copper in it, to give a gold effect. My dad's were all made for him by a brassfounder at Wolverhampton, and he kept them burnished so you'd have sworn they *were* gold. He never let them tarnish, my dad didn't.'

That was the moment when I realized what was wrong with the horse-brass Mary-Lou had found.

'How does brass tarnish?' I asked.

'Gets a kind of green crust on it. Called verdigris.'

'Mr Oakley,' I said, 'that horse-brass came out of the water bright and shining.'

That was the biggest shock yet for Ben Oakley. It staggered us, too. We all understood what it meant. It meant you could bet a pound to a penny that the so-called horse-brass, with the eye in the middle and the sun in splendour around it, was really made of gold. Mary-Lou had been right all along. And Reuben Oakley had had 'a few' of them. Most likely the others were the same.

'I never thought of it,' said Ben, 'but it'd be just like my dad to keep his savings in a form like that. He could see and enjoy them, but with so much imitation gold around, nobody'd guess the brasses were *real* gold.'

'There's probably more of them in the bottom of the boat,' said Brain.

But, you'll hardly believe it, Ben Oakley wasn't looking thrilled.

'I never wanted this,' he said. 'I never wanted anything of my dad's. I've earned a living all my life and I've retired with a bit of capital and my own boat, and I'm satisfied.'

'You mean you won't come to Claypits?' I asked. I was amazed. Wouldn't you have been? Real gold for the picking, maybe, and you could tell he didn't want to have anything to do with it.

After a while he said, sounding reluctant, 'I wouldn't go to Claypits for my own sake, I can tell you that. Not after all these years. And maybe there's nothing else in *Tiddler* anyway, besides what you've found. But if there is, I don't want that Huckle to get his hands on it. And I'd like to see poor old Luke Fillery again. It might be for the last time.'

'So you *will* come,' said Brain. 'We'd like it to be soon. Sooner the better.'

'If I'm coming at all,' said Ben, 'it might as well be now. No time like the present!'

'You mean . . .?' said Brain.

'I mean you can untie that rope and get ready to cast off again. When your home's as portable as mine, you don't have to send for the removal men. I'll tell a couple of neighbours I'm going away for a few days, and we'll be off.'

'Half a minute,' I said. 'What about us? We came on our bikes.'

'Sling them on the roof,' said Ben. 'It's twenty miles to Claypits, and just after two o'clock now. If we break the speed limit a tiny bit, we'll be there about six. Will that do for you?'

That was all right. None of us would be expected home before that time anyway. So ten minutes later the bikes were lying on the cabin roof, where there was plenty of room for them, and *Ellen* was moving out into the basin again. This time we made our way down through the lock into the North-west Junction Canal, with Ben telling us how to work the lock-gear.

'I never thought I'd travel this stretch again,' said Ben as we came out of the lock and started nosing our way along black water between the warehouses and yards and backs of factories that would be the scenery for most of the trip. Ben sighed when he said it. But half a mile farther on he was whistling – a mournful tune, but whistling all the same. He smiled at Sam – rather sadly, perhaps, but it was a smile. And when he went to look for something and left Sam and me side by side at the tiller, Sam nudged me and said, 'It was him and your gran, you know, that were sweethearts all those years ago.'

'What?' I said. I couldn't imagine Gran as anybody's sweetheart.

'Course they were! You are *slow*! She was the girl his dad didn't want him to marry. And after all the trouble she married your gramp instead. But Ben still loved her. Why do you think he called his boat *Ellen*? He called it after *her*, you thickie!'

'Oh,' I said. Well, I reckon Sam had to be right. I mean, it couldn't just be an accident that Ben called his boat the same name, could it? But fancy anyone naming a boat after our gran! Mind you, I can remember Mum saying she wasn't always the old battleaxe she is now.

'He'll be hoping to see her again!' said Sam. '*That's* why he's coming back to Claypits!'

'That, and the Huckles, and the horse-brass, and the money if there is any, and seeing Luke Fillery,' I said.

'Yes,' said Sam. 'It adds up to a lot of reasons, doesn't it?'

'Well, anyway, he's coming, that's the main thing,' I said. And then Ben Oakley reappeared, still whistling, and I guessed that even if he didn't care too much what might be found in his dad's old boat, maybe after all he wasn't *too* reluctant to be heading back to Claypits and all he'd left behind him.

10

It was a great trip back to Claypits. Mind you, it wasn't exactly what you'd call scenic. Claypits is at one end of a conurbation and Southerly Junction's at the other. A conurbation means there's a whole bunch of towns so close together that you don't know when you've left one and moved into the next. And the North-west Junction Canal goes through the grimiest part of every town in the bunch.

But, like I said, it was a great trip. We all had turns at steering the boat and opening and closing the locks. Ben Oakley didn't interfere, except once or twice when we got into a spot of bother. He gave us biscuits and fruit and bars of chocolate to keep us going. And we made pretty good time. Ben had guessed right. It was just about six o'clock when we came alongside the Town Quay at Claypits. We did it in real style. Sam was at the tiller, and she brought the boat in slow and easy so that it just slid gently alongside, and I jumped off with a rope at the back and Brain at the front, and we tied up to the mooring-rings, and Ben watched us and said we were like professionals, nearly. There were about a dozen of the local kids watching, and you could tell they were impressed, and I bet they wished they were us.

There were a couple of things we weren't too pleased to see, though. One was that the scrap-metal boat was tied up a bit further along the quay. So Rick and Roddy were still around. I didn't like that. The other thing was that our own little boat wasn't there any more. We'd been keeping it tied to the railings,

87

and I didn't think for a moment that anyone would have stolen it. I thought most likely Dad had sold it. I'd have gone and asked him, but I knew he'd have closed the workshop doors by now and gone with Brain's dad for a pint before supper.

Unlike us, Ben Oakley was glad to see the scrap-metal boat. 'I want to have a word with those two fellows,' he said, 'and now's as good a time as any. Hang on a minute.'

Brain said, 'They could turn nasty,' but Ben Oakley just grinned. 'With kids, maybe,' he said. 'Somehow I don't think they'll beat *me* up.' And he strode off along the quay. But he was back in less than the minute he'd mentioned. 'The boat's locked up,' he said. 'Nobody aboard.' Then we realized that the little glass-fibre affair with the outboard motor wasn't tied in its usual place at the stern of the scrap-metal boat. Rick and Roddy would have emptied the watered petrol out of the tank by now, that was for sure, and got the boat going again. They must be buzzing around in it somewhere.

Ben Oakley wasn't too disappointed at not getting to talk with them right away. 'There'll be plenty of time,' he said. 'I expect they'll be back here tonight. And I've a pretty good idea what they'll tell me. They'll deny your whole story. They'll say you kids just made it up.'

'Do *you* think we just made it up?' asked Brain.

'No. I believe you. I wouldn't have come all this way if I didn't. But we won't be able to pin anything on them. They'll have sold the things they stole. All I can do is warn them that it's my boat and my land, and they'd better keep out. They'll know who *I* am all right.'

Ben helped us heave our bikes down from the roof. 'You'll be wanting to get home,' he said. 'I'm settling down here for the night. Come and see me tomorrow morning.'

We cycled off up the hill, and the first of our three houses that we came to was Sam's. Sam's mum wasn't back from work yet, and Brain and me decided we could stay for a few minutes, because we were all bursting to talk about Ben and his boat and what was going to happen next. Sam bustled about, putting the supper in the oven to heat up and laying the table, and the three of us all told each other what a good guy Ben was, and what a great boat *Ellen* was. And we were just getting round to the subject of what would happen now when the telephone rang.

Sam answered it. We heard her say 'Hello, Auntie,' and 'Yes, Auntie,' and 'No, Auntie,' and then, in an alarmed tone, 'She isn't here, Auntie.' And then, 'We thought she was staying with you till tonight,' and 'That must have been Darryl,' and 'I've only just come in,' and 'I expect they'll be out playing,' and 'I'll ring you when we've found her.' And then Sam put the phone down and said, sounding really worried, 'Mary-Lou left Auntie's house three hours ago.'

Brain said, 'Your auntie let her go on her own? A little kid her age?'

Sam said, 'No, Auntie says a boy came for her. Said he'd take her home. He looked as if he was about twelve, and Mary-Lou said he was a friend, so Auntie let her go.'

'And you think it was Darryl?' I said.

'Yes. Course it was Darryl. Auntie said his clothes were poor but he seemed harmless. Who else could it be? You know what pals Mary-Lou and Darryl are.'

'Well, she won't come to any harm with Darryl,' I said. 'He'll look after her, same as he did on Tom Tiddler's Ground.'

Then we all stared at one another, and you could bet we'd all had the same thought at once.

'That's where they'll be!' said Brain. 'Tom Tiddler's Ground! She was mad keen to go there again!'

'And that's where our boat'll be!' I said.

It was Sam who had the really scary thought. 'P'raps it's

where Rick and Roddy are, too!' she said. And then, sounding fierce and frightened at the same time, 'I *bet* that's where Rick and Roddy are!'

I felt kind of panicky in my stomach. I told myself this was daft. Mary-Lou and Darryl were just a couple of kids out playing somewhere, and it was broad daylight, and they hadn't been away all that long, and they couldn't have come to any harm. And yet . . . I had a horrid feeling that Sam's guess was right.

'So what are we going to *do* about it?' asked Sam.

Brain said, 'We're going back to the Town Quay. We'll get Ben Oakley to go along there in *Ellen*.'

I said, 'Ben'll be cooking his supper. He's a grown-up. We'll have to *persuade* him. He won't be in a hurry. He'll tell us not to panic.'

Brain said, 'I reckon *I* can persuade him.'

Sam said, 'If we went by land, we'd be halfway there already.' Which was true, because Tom Tiddler's Ground wasn't nearly as far by land as it was by water. But it was an obstacle race getting to it. And I said so. But Sam said, speaking very fast, that it didn't take three of us to persuade Ben Oakley to take the boat along, and Brain should go down to the quay to do that, seeing he was best at talking to grown-ups, while Sam and me went straight to Tom Tiddler's Ground overland.

Brain didn't argue. He set off for the quay. Sam said to me, 'My mum'll be on her way home from work by now, but there isn't time to wait for her.' So she wrote a note to say she'd gone to find Mary-Lou and if her mum wanted to know anything more she must ring Auntie Carol. And Sam and me set off at a run for Tom Tiddler's Ground. We didn't bother to take the bikes. There wasn't any point. The distance was nothing much. The problem was the Throughway.

We knew the district pretty well, of course. We knew which streets and alleyways to take, and where you could cut off a corner by slipping through between rows of houses or across somebody's yard. It was only two or three minutes before we were passing the old slaughterhouse and the canal company premises.

A bit further on, the street system came to a stop. Ahead of us was a high embankment, with the Throughway running along the top of it, as far as you could see in either direction. The railway lines and the canal went under the Throughway in tunnels, but the streets didn't. When the Throughway came, they'd just been cut off. Tom Tiddler's Ground was at the far side of the Throughway, out of sight, and there was only one way we could get to it. Over the top.

Where the street ended, on the face of the embankment, there were warning signs. NO ACCESS. NO TRESPASS-ING. NO PEDESTRIANS ON THE THROUGH-WAY. DANGER! And, in case this wasn't enough to put you off, a high barbed-wire fence. It would have put *us* off all right if we hadn't been so worried about Mary-Lou and Darryl. But we didn't stop to think. We just went straight ahead.

We managed the barbed wire all right. We're both pretty thin. I held two strands apart for Sam to get through, and she held them for me. Sam got through without a scratch or a tear. I was hooked for a second or two by the back of my shirt, but Sam set me loose.

Next came the embankment. At this point it was grass, al-though a bit further along in each direction, where the rail tracks and the canal went through, it became concrete. Grass was easier to climb on than concrete, but the embankment was as high as a house and nearly as steep. If you got halfway up and then fell or rolled down, you'd go straight into the barbed wire. It wouldn't kill you but it might puncture you a bit.

If we'd gone at the climb head-on, we'd never have made it. But Sam found a way. She went up at an angle, with her side pressed against the grass bank. I followed, close enough to hear

her grousing. 'You need one leg shorter than the other for this,' she said. The last bit was the worst, when there was a long way to fall. But we got to the top and crawled through a wooden fence, and there in front of us was the Throughway.

I'll give you a bit of advice. Don't ever try to cross a road like that. You're out of your tiny mind if you do. It's a wonder I'm here to tell you. The traffic goes like the clappers, and nobody's expecting to see anyone on foot. You couldn't complain if they killed you. Not that you'd be there to do any complaining.

Me and Sam waited on the hard shoulder for a gap in the traffic, but for quite a while there wasn't one. It was going past us non-stop, swoosh swoosh swoosh. If a police car had come along we'd have been stopped, but that didn't happen. In the end we made a dash for it and got to the centre reservation. A climb over the crash barrier. Another wait. Everything was coming the other way now. Drivers were making angry signs at us, and I don't blame them. They were right to be furious. If one car had hit us while we crossed the Throughway, another dozen would have run into the back of it. It'd have been on the News. Pile-up on urban throughway. We were a menace. I'm telling you again, don't ever do it.

We got to the other side. But I still come out in a sweat if I think about it.

We weren't at Tom Tiddler's Ground yet. An arm of the canal, like a deep wide ditch, ran along the foot of the embankment at the side we'd just reached. If we'd tried to scramble down and slipped, we'd have gone straight into the water from a height. If we got safely down the embankment, we'd still have to find a way across. No telling how deep the water was. Lots of mud and weed and litter and green scum.

There was just one way. Farther along, where the main canal came out of its tunnel and the arm we were looking at joined it, there was a stop-lock across the arm. You know what a stop-lock is? It's a kind of gate in the water that can be closed if there's an emergency, like if there was a leak in this derelict arm that would drain the water from the main canal. Anyway, what it amounted to was that there was a narrow beam that you could walk across the top of and get to the other side, if you were lucky.

But first we had to get down to the stop-lock. There was a tiny patch of level ground beside it, but it was at the point beside the tunnel where the grass embankment gave way to concrete. Steep, slippery concrete. The only help we had was a railing along the top. All we could do was grab the bottom rail, lower ourselves through, turn our faces to the wall, hang down as far as we could go, let ourselves drop, and hope for the best.

This time I went first. I hit the ground below with a thud that almost jarred me to pieces, and then nearly rolled into the canal, but somehow I recovered with nothing broken or even bent. Sam was still hanging on to the rail above, so I got myself below her and yelled to her to let go. Sam came down with a rush on top of me, and it was a good job she hardly weighs anything or we'd *both* have been in the water.

We picked ourselves up, shaken and a bit breathless, but none the worse. Next problem, the stop-lock. Seen from close to, it wasn't nice at all. A dark, slippery beam, stained with green slime, and black horrible water on either side of it. We looked at each other and Sam said, 'Me first.' I didn't argue with her. I'd seen Sam trotting around the wrecked barge, as surefooted as a cat. And over she went, quick and confident as you like, and was safe at the other side.

I stood hesitating. I was bothered about my trainers. The soles had worn smooth. I called something to Sam about them, and she yelled, 'Take them off and throw them across.' So I

threw the shoes, one after the other, and Sam caught them. And I was on my way, barefoot.

I was all right for the first half. Very steady, taking it easy, not looking down, placing each foot carefully but keeping straight on without a halt. Then there was a nasty bit where the beam was worn away to a glistening narrow ledge, not even flat. I had to keep going. I stepped on to the narrow part, and as I shifted my weight I felt a slimy cold movement under the sole of my front foot. I was slipping. I brought the back foot forward, hastily, but felt that one slide sideways as well. I'd lost my foothold and I was losing balance, too. I broke into a little trot, throwing myself forward but out of control. My feet lost the beam completely. But I'd got just enough impetus to carry me over the last foot of water, and Sam's arms were grabbing me, and for a moment we both seemed to be going in. And then we were safe on dry land. On Tom Tiddler's Ground.

11

The next stage was like finding your way through a jungle. We
didn't want to stick to the canal bank, because the canal took a
long curve, and the edge of it was marshy anyway. We wanted
to cut straight across Tom Tiddler's Ground to the old barge.
But at first we couldn't even see it. There were high reeds and
rushes, and there were scrawny scrubby little trees and huge
brambles and great thick patches of nettle and dock. Close to
our starting-point and partly overhanging the water was a big
decaying willow that had cracked open and was easy to climb.
Sam shinned up it, and was down again in seconds.

'*Tiddler*'s over there,' she said, pointing a way across the
land. 'And there's somebody around.'

'Who? The kids?'

'Can't see from here. Maybe, maybe not. Come on!'

It was no good worrying about being scratched or stung. We
just shoved our way through the undergrowth, hoping we were
going in the right direction. It seemed to take a long time,
though I don't suppose it was long really, and I wondered if
we'd gone wrong. But we hadn't. The roof of the cabin came
into view, and soon afterwards the whole length of the hull. We
were approaching *Tiddler* sideways on.

And there were two figures in the hull. To be exact, there
was one figure kneeling on a plank that had been laid across it,
and there was another that was right down in the hull, and
only showing the back of its head and shoulders.

Not Darryl and Mary-Lou.

Rick and Roddy.

We stayed, crouched well down in long grass and weeds. They hadn't seen us, and we didn't want them to. We couldn't say anything to each other. We just watched. And listened.

There were kind of swabbing and squelching sounds, and we could see what was making them. Rick and Roddy were sifting through the silt in the hull. Rick was heaving stuff up in a big red plastic bucket, and Roddy was pouring it over the side through some kind of sieve. And it was a filthy job. Even from where we were, we could see they were wet and muddy, and we could hear that they were in a terrible temper. They were swearing away at each other and at the barge and the silt and the water and everything under the sun. We'd have enjoyed it if we hadn't been scared of being seen and worried about Mary-Lou and Darryl. There was no sign of *them*.

Next thing was a splash and a fresh burst of swearing from Rick, and I reckoned he must have slipped and got even wetter. Then both of them climbed out of the hull, sat on the plank, and lit cigarettes. It looked as if they were taking a break. And as if they needed it. Sam and me stayed crouching where we were. A minute or two went by, and Roddy said, 'Come on, then, we better get on with it,' and Rick groused at him and said they were wasting their time.

And then suddenly Roddy stands up on the plank and lets loose a flood of bad language, and him and Rick jump off the far side of the boat and go rushing into the undergrowth twenty or thirty yards to our right. There's a yelp and a scuffle. And we realize that we aren't the only people who've been crawling around and keeping hidden, because Rick and Roddy are heading back to the boat, dragging Darryl and Mary-Lou behind them, and looking madder than ever. And Roddy yells, 'Didn't we tell you to bugger off?' and gives Darryl a clout, and Mary-Lou starts screaming, and Rick roars at Mary-Lou that if she doesn't stop that row he'll murder her, and Darryl

breaks away but Roddy grabs him and Mary-Lou screeches
again and Rick lifts his great ham fist and it looks as if he really
will kill her.

And that blows our cover, because Sam leaps out of the long
grass and rushes at Rick and starts pounding him with her fists,
yelling, 'You let my sister alone!' Rick turns on Sam, and
Mary-Lou starts pounding him from the other side, still
screeching, and Rick turns back again and doesn't seem to
know which of them to start on first. It's as if he was a bull
between two toreadors, and he's about as strong as a bull but
not as bright. Then he makes up his mind and takes a great
swipe at Sam, and Sam dances out of the way and Rick staggers
forward, and Sam shouts to Mary-Lou to run, and Mary-Lou
disappears into the undergrowth and Sam dashes after her,
and Rick has lost them both and turns his attention to Darryl,
who is being held by Roddy in a kind of half-nelson and looks
scared stiff.

You'll be wondering what *I'm* doing while all this is going on. I'm biding my time, that's what I'm doing. Seems to me that kids can't win a fight with two grown men, one of them as big as a house and the other little but wiry and nasty-looking. What I've got to do is help Darryl to get away from them as soon as there's a chance. *If* there's a chance. In another second Rick is going to knock Darryl cold. Could kill him, though he probably doesn't mean to.

But with a quick twisty movement Roddy spins Darryl out of Rick's reach. 'Hold it!' he tells his pal. Doesn't want them to be on a murder charge, I dare say. Then Roddy lets Darryl go, but kind of fixes him with a look, and Darryl doesn't run, he just stands there helpless, as if his legs were going to fold underneath him any second. Talk about a bunny-rabbit and a snake, that's how Darryl is with Roddy. Hypnotized. Can't move.

And Roddy's a lot smarter than Rick. He says to Darryl, quite quiet now and thoughtful, 'We told you an hour ago to buzz off. *Why didn't you go?*'

Darryl just stares at him and doesn't say a word.

'You'd *found* something, hadn't you?' says Roddy. '*That's* why you hung about when you were told to go!'

Darryl stands there with his mouth opening and closing like a goldfish in a bowl and nothing coming out. And suddenly I can recognize his expression. It's a *guilty* one. Like a child being asked by a teacher whether he did something, and not saying anything, but giving himself away by the look on his face.

'Show us!' says Roddy. 'Show us where it is!'

Darryl still doesn't say a word. But he *looks*. He looks sideways towards the roots of the big bramble where Mary-Lou hid the jar of pennies when she first found it. And he looks away again, quick, but that one look has been enough to do the damage. I've got the message, and so has Roddy. Darryl might just as well have said out loud, 'Under the bramble-bush.'

'Stay there!' Roddy tells him. 'Don't move!' And Rick raises a fist to warn him, but I don't think Darryl could move anyway. Roddy is down on his knees already, scrabbling under the bramble-bush. Stretching out an arm. Wincing, because he must be getting scratched. And then a yell of triumph, and Roddy hauls something out from under the bush and lays it out, very carefully, on the ground between himself and Rick. Something that gleams. Or rather, some things that gleam.

I can see quite clearly from where I am. One, two, three, four, five of them, fastened along a blackened strip that must be leather. I can tell from the way Roddy handles it that it's fragile, maybe going to crumble to bits. But there's nothing wrong with the five bright shiners strung along it. Horse-brasses. Not ordinary horse-brasses, though.

'They're gold all right!' Roddy tells Rick. 'And what a weight of it! Worth thousands! Pass me that bag over.'

There's a bag on the grass, the kind that maybe a plumber would carry tools in. Rick hands it over, and Roddy, still very careful, puts the strip of leather with the five gold discs inside, and closes it.

Darryl's still standing there. He isn't going to do anything. He *can't* do anything. I'll have to come out of cover.

Yes, I admit I'm scared. So would you have been. I'm scared stiff. But out I come. Rick and Roddy swivel round and stare at me. And not in a welcoming way.

Rick says, 'Another of that lot! And it *musta* been one of them that put water in our tank. I'll . . .'

'Never mind that now!' says Roddy. To me he says, 'Are there any more of you here?'

'Th-there's only me,' I say.

'Then get out, and be thankful you're in one piece!' says Roddy. Rick is still scowling, and I can hardly speak for fright, but I say, 'I saw what you've got there.'

'*What?*' asks Roddy, very sharp.

'A row of five gold horse-brasses.'

'Gold horse-brasses?' says Roddy, sarcastic. 'What were they in – a fairy tale? Go on, get out of here. And' – pointing at Darryl – 'take him with you!'

I say, standing my ground, 'They're not yours. They belong to Ben Oakley. He owns the boat and the land.'

'Ben Oakley, eh?' says Roddy. 'You been doing some homework, ain't you? This *was* Ben Oakley's boat, once. Long ago. But he's not been seen around here for donkeys' years.'

'He's on his way now,' I say. I'm trying hard to sound more assured than I feel. 'He came down this afternoon from Southerly Junction in his own canal-boat. He'll be here any minute. You'll have to hand the horse-brasses over.'

And now Roddy smiles.

'Horse-brasses?' he says. 'I don't know what you're talking about. We haven't got any horse-brasses.'

'B-but you have!' says Darryl, getting his voice back at last. 'They're in that bag! I saw you put them there! Me and Mary-Lou found them in the bottom of the barge!'

'Kids' tales!' says Roddy. He sounds confident. '*I've* not seen no horse-brasses, have *you*, Rick?'

Rick looks baffled, then catches on and says, 'No, Roddy.'

And I can see why Roddy's confident. He'll get rid of his loot double-quick, and if anything comes out it'll be our word against his and Rick's. Probably no one will take us seriously anyway. We're only a bunch of kids.

But it's just at that minute that I hear, from a long way off, a sound that I recognize at once because I've been hearing it all afternoon. It's the sound of a diesel engine, and I know what it comes from. It's from Ben's boat *Ellen*.

Rick and Roddy have heard it too. 'Look over there!' says Rick to Roddy. I look the way he's pointing, across Tom Tiddler's Ground towards the tunnel that brings the canal under the Throughway. I can't see any boat yet. But just this side of the tunnel, in the big decayed willow at the water's edge, there's Sam, crouched crazily on a branch, waving a purple object. It's Mary-Lou's woolly jumper. Anyone can see that Sam's signalling to somebody.

'Hell!' says Roddy. 'Could be trouble. Come on, Rick, we got nothing to stay here for anyway. Let's go!' He picks up the bag. Rick looks as if he'd like to give Darryl and me a clout before they go, just for luck, but Roddy won't have it, and in a moment they're hurrying off down the side of the inlet to where their little boat must be tied up. I yell to Darryl to follow me, and we head away in a different direction – overland across Tom Tiddler's Ground towards the tunnel and the tree and Sam.

It's hard going through the undergrowth, but we're cutting off a big bend in the canal, and I belt ahead as fast as I can with my heart thumping like mad, and I can hear Darryl panting along behind me. Halfway across, we hear behind us the sound of an outboard motor being started. Twice it fails. The third time it fires. Rick and Roddy are sure to come this way, because there's less than half a mile of canal in the other direction before it ends. They'll try to get past Ben before he knows what's happening.

We come out on the canal bank right beside the tree, with Sam still leaning out and waving the woolly and Mary-Lou on the ground, jumping up and down. And just as we arrive, *Ellen* comes out of the tunnel. Brain's standing in the bow, and he reacts right away to Sam's signal. He grabs a rope and perches on the edge, ready to jump ashore. Ben Oakley, steering from the back, puts the helm across. They can see that all four of us are here, and they're going to land and pick us up.

But that's not what's wanted now. Rick and Roddy in the little glass-fibre dinghy are already in view, coming on steadily towards *Ellen*. Looks like they'll get past and be away through the tunnel, and nobody will see them again until they've turned those brasses into cash.

As Sam comes down from the tree, I signal even more wildly and point in the direction of the little boat, now putting on speed. I point again and again and bawl at the top of my voice, 'Stop them!' And I've got to hand it to Brain. He didn't get called that for nothing. He's quick on the uptake. He's signalling with outstretched arm for Ben to move right. So am I. So, now, is Darryl. Brain's yelling, and Ben has a hand cupped to his ear, and Roddy and Rick are still coming on. They're going to get past.

And then Ben gets the message. He shoves the tiller across. The bow of the canal-boat comes hard round, pointing for the far bank. The back end, with Ben and the propeller, swings round towards us.

Ellen is longer than the canal is wide, and can close it off. Rick and Roddy can see that as well as we can. Roddy, at the wheel, puts on a spurt. The front end of *Ellen* has touched the far bank. No getting past on that side. Roddy changes course and shoots in towards the near bank, aiming at the gap between the back end of *Ellen* and the bank. But the back end is still swinging round, and the gap is narrowing. It's touch-and-go whether the little boat gets through.

Looks like she'll make it, just. She's going at her top speed and the gap's closing slowly as *Ellen*'s propeller labours to push seventy-two feet of canal-boat sideways on. Rick and Roddy will get through. No, they won't. Yes, they will. They won't. Suddenly the back rail of *Ellen* is right here, almost in our faces. There's a great thump as she hits the bank, a grinding noise from the prop, and the tiller is jerked from Ben Oakley's hands. But *Ellen* has done the trick. The canal is blocked. And instead of sneaking through the gap, the little boat has rammed the canal-boat's rear end.

Ever thought what happens to a flimsy glass-fibre dinghy if it runs at top speed into the eighteen-ton metal hull of a canal-boat? I don't suppose you have. No reason why you should.

Well, I'll tell you. It breaks like an eggshell. In a split second, the bow is stove in and the little boat is filling with water. In a few more seconds, Rick and Roddy are struggling in the canal. Ben Oakley's put *Ellen* out of gear, because he doesn't want the prop to chop them into mincemeat. We're all helping them out, and nearly falling in ourselves, and I don't know why we bother, because they're not a bit grateful. They're swearing at us and at Ben, and Ben's swearing back. We've told Ben who they are – as if he hadn't guessed – and he's cursing them for being suicidal maniacs as well as thugs. Roddy is hanging on to the bag with the horse-brasses, and it looks as if it'll go down and maybe Roddy with it, until I grab it from him and heave it on board *Ellen*, quick. And when a sodden Roddy crawls up on to the bank, Ben's standing right there in front of him, telling him not to start any trouble.

It takes all the rest of us to get Rick out. He's half drowned, choking and gasping. Somehow we heave him on to the bank,

and he lies there waterlogged, drawing great noisy gulps of breath.

Roddy doesn't give a damn about Rick. He's carrying on something unbelievable against Ben, demanding his bag back and threatening to sue him for the value of the dinghy, and telling him a dozen horrible things he's going to do to him, to say nothing of what he's going to do to *us*. But he's chosen the wrong man for that sort of talk. Ben Oakley may be getting on in years, but he's tough and fit and he did some boxing when he was young. And when Roddy's finished pouring out threats, Ben says, 'All right. What are you going to do about *this*?' And he lets loose a piledriver to the jaw, and down goes Roddy. All that's missing is a referee to count him out.

'Come on, kids! All aboard!' says Ben. He jumps Mary-Lou on to the back deck of the canal-boat and the rest of us follow.

'Throw the fellow's bag ashore!' Ben tells me. So I give him the good news about the horse-brasses, and Ben says yes, they must be his dad's, and yes, they must belong to *him* now, and yes, I can take them out and put them on the cabin table before I throw Roddy his bag with whatever else may be in it, but the plain fact is that Ben's not all that excited by our finds and is more interested in getting the boat moving again. He starts up the engine and backs *Ellen* off the bank, and the front end swings round and we move forward. Roddy is raising his head off the ground, slowly and painfully, and Rick is still gulping air, and they haven't even the energy to swear.

'Make your own way home!' Ben tells them cheerfully as we slide past. We can't turn *Ellen* round, because as I said she's longer than the canal is wide, so we have to go on to the end of the canal at the East Basin. Then we turn and head back for the Town Quay. We look out for Rick and Roddy, but by now they've managed to pick themselves up and take themselves off, and the only trace of them is a bit of floating wreckage from their boat.

'*Will* they sue you?' Brain asks Ben Oakley, but Ben just laughs and says, 'You bet they won't!' Then, at last, Ben asks Brain to take the tiller, and comes into the cabin with us to look at the brasses. They're still on the strip of leather, though it looks as if it'll come to pieces at a touch, and oh boy, do they look good! Mary-Lou is dancing around, bursting with excitement and all agog to tell Ben how clever she is. '*I* found them!' she says. 'Well, me and Darryl found them, but it was me that knew they'd be found!' And she sets up her chant at the top of her voice:

'Here we come on Tom Tiddler's Ground,
 Picking up gold and silver!
 Picking up gold and sil-ver!
 Here we come on Tom Tiddler's Ground,
 Picking up gold and sil-ver!'

12

There's quite a lot I haven't told you. Sometimes everything's happening at once, like it was that evening, but if you're writing it down you can only say one thing at a time. So I couldn't tell you how, while Sam and me were making our way to Tom Tiddler's Ground, Brain was belting down to the Town Quay and persuading Ben Oakley to start up *Ellen* and come along the canal after us. Brain said Ben took quite a bit of persuading. But that's another problem. How would I know? I wasn't there. I can't be in two places at once, can I? I've written it the best I could. I bet you wouldn't have managed it any better.

Anyway, after that it all eased off a bit. Things had happened so quickly that we got back to Sam's house soon after her mum did, and her mum was actually on the phone to her Auntie Carol about Mary-Lou's disappearance, and she just said, 'Oh, here they are,' quite calm, and gave Sam and Mary-Lou a ticking-off, and that was all. Mary-Lou went on chattering for weeks about the horsy things she'd found, but her mum just thought it was Mary-Lou romancing, and didn't take much notice.

Yes, I know, you want to hear about the horse-brasses. Well, they were gold all right. They were a different pattern from the first one Mary-Lou had found. They had pictures of horses on them, with names like 'Captain' and 'Tinker' engraved underneath, and Ben reckoned that these were horses his dad had owned in the old days. Being made of gold, the 'brasses' would be worth a fortune nowadays, Ben thought, but he didn't want it. He gave the set of five to a waterways museum, and they're still on show there. The museum people managed to preserve the strap they were on, which was called a martingale and was the part of the harness that goes down from a horse's collar between its forelegs, and was a favourite place for hanging brasses on.

I dare say you've been wondering about Ben and my gran, too. Well, within a day or two of getting back to Claypits, Ben went to tea at Gran's. That's another thing I can't tell you much about, because I wasn't there. But Mum said Gran brought out the salmon for Ben, and that must mean something. Ben's gone to Gran's house a good few times since then, and she's been on board his canal-boat, and Dad saw him taking a photo of her on the Town Quay with the name ELLEN on the boat just behind her.

Dad reckons Ben and Gran are courting again, after all these years. Honest. No kidding. Courting, at their age! My mum says it's never too late and maybe she'd get on better with Gran if she saw a bit less of her. I must admit, the old girl's a lot better-tempered than she used to be.

Then there was Ben's visit to Luke Fillery at Peaceholme. Ben was very modest about it afterwards, but I reckon a visit from him was the biggest treat that poor old Luke had had for a long time. And soon afterwards Luke had another treat, because we'd told Ben how Luke had this wish for one more trip on the canals, and Ben kind of borrowed him from Peaceholme and took him on a three-week round trip on the canal network, and the weather stayed good and Luke had a great time, but Ben reckons that by the time it was over Luke had had enough and was quite glad to come back to Peaceholme, and he's satisfied now and says he'll die happy.

What with seeing Gran and Luke and getting to know *us*, Ben changed his mind about being in Claypits. He came back from Southerly Junction to Tom Tiddler's Ground and moored his boat beside his own land, and he's still there except when he's away on a trip. He's taking Tom Tiddler's Ground in hand and cutting down the scrub and so on, and he's also breaking up the old boat, because he reckons she's so far gone she's nothing now but an eyesore. We all wondered if there might still be more horse-brasses or other treasures in the silt at the bottom of the hull, but Ben pumped it all out and didn't find anything, and I don't think he was sorry. Rick and Roddy are still working the scrap-metal boat, and they turn up in Claypits from time to time, but they always give Ben a wide berth and they don't bother us. He didn't hear anything more about the wreck of their dinghy. Served them right, say I.

Me and Brain and Sam have gone on from Claypits Primary to the Comprehensive. It's all right, once you've got used to moving from the top of one school to the bottom of another. Brain is living up to his name. He's good at just about every subject you can think of. Sam's making her mark, too. She's a First-year Representative on the School Council, and she doesn't half take it seriously. I wouldn't be surprised if she finishes up as Prime Minister. If you can make it from a grocer's shop in Grantham, why not from a back street in Claypits? Me, I guess I'm just ordinary, and that has its points. People don't expect too much of you, and then they're not disappointed.

Mary-Lou's new front teeth are fully grown and make her look older. She doesn't cling to Sam the way she used to, now they're at different schools. She's got a whole lot of pals of her own. So far as I can see, she bosses them all around. But Mary-Lou won't even speak to *me*. Boys are silly, she says. The only exception she'll make is for Darryl. Poor old Darryl. Mary-Lou likes him, and Ben Oakley says he has more to him than people think. But I reckon that whatever happens, kids like Darryl stay at the bottom of the heap, and Darryl knows it himself. Nobody expects anything from him, and he doesn't expect anything from anyone.

My dad hasn't sold the little boat we first went to Tom Tiddler's Ground in. We won't let him. We still need it, we tell him. He can sell it when me and Brain have finished the new little boat we're building (with a bit of help from Brain's dad). It's taking longer than we thought, but it's going to be a lovely job. We haven't told Ben Oakley about it. It'll be a surprise for him. We thought of naming it *Tiddler the Second*, but that didn't seem quite right. We're going to call it *Whale*.